FALL IN LOVE WITH
THE MARRIAGE TO A BILLIONAIRE
SERIES!

"It's always been you. I don't want anybody else; I don't dream about anybody else. It's only you." –Nick to Alexa, *The Marriage Bargain*

"For someone to hurt you like this makes me question what is fair and right in this world. But you, *mia amore*, took such an event and gained strength. You made your life on your own terms with no one to help. You humble me." –Michael to Maggie, *The Marriage Trap*

"And as for cooking, I am doing this for one reason. Every woman should know how to make one signature dessert. Not for anyone else but herself. Now, mix." –Mama Conte to Maggie, *The Marriage Trap*

"You need to be strong on your own before you can be strong with someone else." –Mama Conte to Carina, *The Marriage Mistake*

"Did you ever think I want more than any man can handle?" The brave words lost a bit of impact as he tugged on her earlobe and a breathy gasp escaped. "All this time, you've been wrong, Max. It's not me who can't handle them." She smiled up at him in pure challenge. "They can't handle me." –Max and Carina, *The Marriage Mistake*

"You offer me an apology?" he tore out, golden eyes spitting sparks of fiery rage as he shook her slightly. "You think I'm upset because I'm stuck with you? How dare you call yourself a charity case to the man who kissed you and stripped you and fucked you for so many hours we both fell into exhaustion? You deserve a man to be whole—a man who can offer you a decent life and not tear you apart piece by piece. I'll never be able to give you what you need. Don't you understand I'm frozen inside? There's nothing left to give you except physical pleasure." –Sawyer to Julietta, *The Marriage Merger*

She rose and came to him. Strong arms held him with no apology, no hesitation. She stroked his hair like a mother would, soothing him with her warmth and safety and beliefs. "My sweet boy, yes, you can. Your life is your own. You were a child and could not protect the ones you loved. None of us can. So instead, we choose to love as much as possible, and that needs to be enough." –Mama Conte to Sawyer, *The Marriage Merger*

The Marriage Arrangement

Also from Jennifer Probst

The Billionaire Builders
Everywhere and Every Way
Any Time, Any Place
All Or Nothing At All

Searching for Series:
Searching for Someday
Searching for Perfect
Searching for Beautiful
Searching for Always
Searching for You

The Marriage to a Billionaire series:
The Marriage Bargain
The Marriage Trap
The Marriage Mistake
The Marriage Merger
The Books of Spells

Executive Seduction

All the Way

The Sex on the Beach Series:
Beyond Me
Chasing Me

The Hot in the Hamptons Series:
Summer Sins

The Steele Brother Series:
Catch Me
Play Me
Dare Me

Beg Me
Reveal Me

Dante's Fire
The Grinch of Starlight Bend

The Marriage Arrangement

A Marriage to a Billionaire Novella

By Jennifer Probst

1001 Dark Nights

EVIL EYE
CONCEPTS

The Marriage Arrangement
A Marriage to a Billionaire Novella
By Jennifer Probst

1001 Dark Nights

Copyright 2018 Triple J Publishing Inc
ISBN: 978-1-948050-25-8

Foreword: Copyright 2014 M. J. Rose

Published by Evil Eye Concepts, Incorporated

Acknowledgments from the Author

Thanks to the 1001 Dark Nights team for everything they do. I'm honored to be included in such a wonderful organization who support their authors and make them feel so valued. From the editing, to the marketing, and everything in between – you all make publishing a book such a pleasure.

Dedication

I'd like to thank two special people who've made a difference.

First, Liz Berry. You reached out to me during an extremely difficult time and gave me hope I'd not only get through the grief, but would be able to write again. Your support and love meant the world to me and I will never forget it.

Second, Wendy S. Marcus. You answered my cry for help and got me through this book with your honest feedback and willingness to edit a first draft. You've been with me from the beginning and I'm lucky to call you my friend. Thank you so much.

Sign up for the 1001 Dark Nights Newsletter
and be entered to win a Tiffany Key necklace.

There's a contest every month!

Go to www.1001DarkNights.com to subscribe.

One Thousand and One Dark Nights

Once upon a time, in the future...

*I was a student fascinated with stories and learning.
I studied philosophy, poetry, history, the occult, and
the art and science of love and magic. I had a vast
library at my father's home and collected thousands
of volumes of fantastic tales.*

*I learned all about ancient races and bygone
times. About myths and legends and dreams of all
people through the millennium. And the more I read
the stronger my imagination grew until I discovered
that I was able to travel into the stories... to actually
become part of them.*

*I wish I could say that I listened to my teacher
and respected my gift, as I ought to have. If I had, I
would not be telling you this tale now.
But I was foolhardy and confused, showing off
with bravery.*

*One afternoon, curious about the myth of the
Arabian Nights, I traveled back to ancient Persia to
see for myself if it was true that every day Shahryar
(Persian: شهريار, "king") married a new virgin, and then
sent yesterday's wife to be beheaded. It was written
and I had read, that by the time he met Scheherazade,
the vizier's daughter, he'd killed one thousand
women.*

Something went wrong with my efforts. I arrived in the midst of the story and somehow exchanged places with Scheherazade – a phenomena that had never occurred before and that still to this day, I cannot explain.

Now I am trapped in that ancient past. I have taken on Scheherazade's life and the only way I can protect myself and stay alive is to do what she did to protect herself and stay alive.

Every night the King calls for me and listens as I spin tales. And when the evening ends and dawn breaks, I stop at a point that leaves him breathless and yearning for more. And so the King spares my life for one more day, so that he might hear the rest of my dark tale.

As soon as I finish a story... I begin a new one... like the one that you, dear reader, have before you now.

Prologue

"All endings are also beginnings. We just don't know it at the time." – *Mitch Albom*

"You have to marry her."

Rip Savage stared at the man who'd been like a father to him over the past year. Even now, with worry lines bracketing his eyes and mouth, the older man retained a sense of elegance and grace befitting someone of English descent, even royalty. With his thinning silver hair, thick black framed glasses, and penchant for designer black suits, he cut an intimidating figure, even before one stared into those pale blue eyes that could turn steel grey with stubborn defiance. Of course, Edward Winsor had a reputation to live up to. Within the cliques of vineyards and winery owners in the Hudson Valley, he was well known for his quality vintage and a tightly knit family-run business that competed with Brotherhood Winery for the oldest run winery in the state. His estate was small but mighty, and one of the sought-after blue-bloods that many admired.

Rip had been the only one to know Winsor Winery had been almost bankrupt. Beneath the flawless surface, something rotten had flourished. When Rip was hired to pull the business from ruin, he'd been focused on success no matter what the cost. He hadn't expected to develop such affection for Edward, or be treated like a son rather than a hired associate.

Therefore, instead of panic, he regarded the older man from across his cherrywood desk with a frown. "I don't understand. What does Caterina have to do with the winery?"

Edward gave a long sigh, tapping his elegant finger against the etched crystal highball glass that contained his usual two fingers of Scotch. He shifted his weight in his chair, causing the leather to squeak slightly. They were in Rip's favorite room—the library/study—decorated in bold, rich wines with a hint of Tuscan gold. The fabrics were decadent, from the expensive dark leathers to the Oriental tapestry rugs, and burgundy velvet couches. Bookshelves lined the wall, the scents of old paper and leather bindings with a touch of wood polish drifting in the air. The large bay windows overlooked the acres of rolling property with the view of the spectacular Shawangunk Mountains.

Usually, the view alone soothed him. Reminded him of his success and how far he'd come in a world he'd fought to break into. But his nerves were edged with a fine tension that matched his gut. Something bad was going down, and he had a terrible idea he wouldn't be able to stop it.

"I'm sorry to be so mysterious, Rip. The bottom line is, I'm ready to retire. My health is deteriorating, and the doctor advised if I don't get to a warmer climate, I'll be pushing my odds. I love this life but it's time to move on."

Rip nodded. "You warned me about this months ago. I'm ready for the challenge. I've proved I can run Winsor Winery successfully. We can sign the contracts immediately and I'll help settle you wherever you choose."

Regret flashed in the man's blue eyes. "You saved my business, and deserve to inherit control. But I can't do it, Rip. Winsor Winery can only be given to a family member. No matter how much I love you like my son, you're not blood."

His body numbed. The past reared up—ugly and telling—reminding him once again he'd always be an outsider. There was no such thing as a reward for hard work, or fairness. There was only the same lesson he'd learned time and time again.

He belonged to no one.

He was alone.

"You can do anything you want," Rip said. "You're choosing to deny me my rights, even after I was promised full control after your daughter ran out on you."

Edward took off his glasses and rubbed his nose. "I know. I made a mistake. I contacted my lawyer when I realized I'd need to step down, and was reminded that part of the clause from generations ago was that the winery and land stays in the family. It can't be sold outside the Winsor name."

"And if you had no children to inherit?" Rip asked.

"Control reverts to a sibling, and the oldest niece or nephew."

A curse blistered past his lips. He jammed his hands in his pockets and tried to make sense of the mess unfolding. "Your daughter wants nothing to do with the business. She ran away to play in Italy, not caring you were near financial disaster. How can you leave it to her to be destroyed?"

Edward raised his head. Steely resolve glowed in his blue eyes. "I've been thinking about this a long time, Rip. You're like a son to me. You deserve to be part of Winsor Winery. And from the time my daughter was an infant, I've raised her with one goal in mind: to eventually run the family business. But perhaps I pushed too hard." The older man's shoulders sagged. "After she lost her fiancé, she swore to carve out a new life for herself. But it's time for her to stop running. This land is part of her blood. You're a good man, and Caterina is your perfect match. With you both at the helm, you would make an incredible team."

A humorless laugh escaped Rip. He shook his head and began pacing. "You're suggesting an arranged marriage in order to gain a business? I'm either trapped in the Middle Ages or caught in an awful Hollywood chick flick. This is insane. We've never even met. She'd never agree."

"I think this business means more to her than she thinks. If it's a matter of losing her home and inheritance, she may agree to the terms."

He narrowed his gaze. "You'd allow your daughter to marry someone she doesn't love? Force her into an arrangement in order to satisfy some ancient clause that can probably be broken, or challenged?"

"There is no negotiation on the clause—I've already checked. I'm not about to force my daughter to do anything. But I think you would be good for Cat," he added softly. "You're a man with a rare quality that is integral to her happiness."

Bitterness tinged his tone. "What's that?"

"Loyalty. Honor."

The words singed him like flames. He got up, pacing the room like a caged, pissed-off tiger. "And me? You have no problem sacrificing my wants or happiness for this end game?"

The man's sigh drifted to his ears. "I knew you'd be pissed off. Feel betrayed. You may not believe me right now, but I love both of you. I'm simply looking for a way where everyone wins. You get the winery, I get to retire, and you both get the opportunity to win something bigger. Love."

"Love? Forgive me, Edward, but the only thing your daughter and I have in common is this winery. There will be no love between us. Just responsibility. Is that what you want?"

"I want something more for both of you. I've watched you this past year, Rip. You're thirty-five years old with no ties to this world. You deserve more than this type of life you pretend is enough, and Cat may be exactly what you're missing. She's spirited, and intelligent, and though she swore she was done with the winery, she still has a deep love for this place. It's time to bring her home and for a new generation to begin. That's my hope for all this. And though it may appear ruthless, and you may never forgive me, I'm willing to take that risk."

He threw out his final challenge. "And if she disagrees? If I fail to convince her marriage to a stranger is the only solution?"

Edward's jaw clenched. "Then I'll continue to work here even if my doctor disapproves. When I die, it will be automatically willed to her as in the terms of the agreement."

Silence fell.

Rip spun away. His lungs emptied of air as he struggled to understand the betrayal of a man he'd trusted. The late afternoon sunlight streamed through the oversized bay windows, wrapping the room in golden light. He watched the effect the sunbeams had on the office. Swirling tendrils of pain and emptiness ripped at his insides, fighting to get out, but he forced them back, his many years of discipline winning over his temptation to let the emotions run rampant.

Odd that as angry as he was, he felt the bitterness more intently; that the past year as Edward's right-hand man and friend meant nothing. Rip couldn't take over the family business because he wasn't family. All his work, care, and sacrifice to bring the winery back from bankruptcy didn't matter. Blood mattered.

Once again, Rip found himself chasing a prize that danced just out of reach, like the shadow chased the elusive light of the sun.

And once again, he found himself back in the darkness.

So be it.

He swiveled on his heel and schooled his face to show no emotion. The ending was clear to him, and there was no doubt he'd win. He'd learned the lesson early, trapped in an abusive home, craving a life that was bigger and better and beyond reach. Sometimes, he believed he'd gotten there, only to realize it had only been a mirage—like now.

None of it mattered. He wanted Winsor Winery for himself. If the only way to do it was to marry a rich, spoiled heiress, he'd do it. If he had to make her fall in love with him, he would. If he had to lie, or deceive, he would. And by God, he'd have no blood on his hands because it was her own father who'd forced his hand.

"Where is she?"

"In Milan. I'll give you her address."

He gave a curt nod. "Don't let her know I'm coming. I'd prefer to do this on my own, without any interference."

Edward looked torn. "She deserves to hear the truth from me."

"Then give me at least a week. Give me some time to get to know her before you bring up the idea of marriage. I'd like to see if we can even make this work between us."

Slowly, the older man nodded. "One week. Then I'll call and explain everything. If you both feel you can't go through with it, I'll accept your resignation."

"Fine. I'll go make the arrangements." He swiveled on his heel but the sound of his name made him pause. "Yes?"

"I know you don't believe me now, but I'm doing what I believe is best. For both of you."

A thousand different responses rose to his lips, but Rip bit them all back, leaving Edward Winsor alone in silence.

It was time to go meet his future wife.

Chapter One

This was *so* embarrassing.

Caterina looked around her apartment and prayed no one would ever find out. Unless there were hidden cameras planted, or she'd suddenly become famous on TMZ, her shameful secret should be safe. But it came at a high price.

Humiliation for the female species.

With a groan, she did the deed and dropped the handwritten paper into the small fire she'd created in a kitchen pot. As the flames ate up and spit out burnt pieces, she reminded herself creating a love spell to find her soulmate was an extremely healthy thing to do.

Over a year ago, she'd arrived in Italy devastated. Heartbroken. Her entire life had blown up a week before her planned extravagant wedding, and she'd left everything behind to carve out a new life for herself. One without her being dependent on any man—including her father. One on her own terms.

Now, she'd finally found some vestige of happiness and it was time to venture into the dating pool again. She missed men—from their musky scent to their hard muscles, sexy smiles, and confident swaggers. She missed the rough touch of a hand on hers, and the powerful way they'd guide her under an elbow to gently lead. She missed the thrill of a first kiss, lips tentatively sliding over hers before his tongue slid masterfully inside to stroke and pleasure.

She missed sex.

Badly.

But she wasn't yet ready for dating sites, or match-ups by well-meaning friends who had no clue what she was looking for. She'd stumbled on the violet, fabric covered Book of Spells while antiquing in Milan. The moment her fingers closed around the worn spine, she'd experienced a jolt of anticipation. It was even written in English—a real find when most books were Italian. The spell was quite simple—make a list of all the qualities one needed in a soulmate, chant a quick spell to Earth Mother, and burn the piece of paper in fire. Place a second copy of the list under her mattress. Then wait for Mr. Right.

Yeah, so much better than Tinder.

She glanced at the list for the final time to make sure she hadn't missed anything.

1. A man who is passionate and madly in love with her.
2. A hard worker
3. A man with great loyalty
4. A man who makes her feel safe
5. A man who is tender
6. A man who supports and believes in her
7. A man with character
8. A man who loves her father
9. A man who makes her believe in love again
10. A man who isn't afraid to give her all of himself
11. A man who rocks her world in bed

Yes, it was a perfect list. Shaking her head, she shoved the paper under her mattress, cleaned up the mess, and put the book on the table. At least she felt as if she had done something to further her goal. A first step was crucial toward getting what one desired, as her father used to say. A pang of loneliness hit her when she thought of him, running Winsor Winery alone. When she'd walked in on her fiancé, Devon, screwing one of the tasting clients right before their wedding, she'd lost a future husband and Papa had lost a partner. Papa had been forced to go outside their tight-knit world to hire a new assistant. From his emails, though, it seemed her father had made the right choice with Ripley Savage. And yet he continued to beg her to come home to take over the business where, in his opinion, she belonged.

Unfortunately, she wasn't ready to return to the scene of her heartbreak, and had been too cowardly to tell her father the truth.

There was a good chance she'd never be ready.

Guilt consumed her. Her entire life had revolved around a business that had been as much a part of her as her next breath. Through good and bad seasons, the grapes and her father had been her only constants.

But she'd never known anything else, had never had the choice of a different life.

The moment she'd tasted freedom, Cat realized the endless possibilities that lay before her, so she wanted nothing more to do with making wine. She'd steeped herself in travel, finally deciding to try her hand at designing and creating purses to see if she could eventually launch a successful business of her own. She'd taken classes, immersed herself in fine leathers and textiles, visiting endless purse designers to study, and felt on the brink of being able to finally begin.

Cat glanced at some of her samples, piled high on the small table. The studio apartment located in the expensive Brera district of Milano was small, but functional. Sure, the kitchen had a barely working stove and no dishwasher, but the ceilings soared high and the oversized windows allowed sun to pour in. The walls were bright yellow, the floors a warm pine, and the small wrought iron terrace gave her the outdoor space she craved. Thank goodness she didn't need to cook. Besides, why cook in Italy when she could sample the amazing array of delights at her fingertips? Cat trusted the professionals. She'd made a ton of friends from her regular routine of eating out, and it was more fun than slaving in her nonexistent kitchen trying to make boxed pasta.

The small television got a few channels, but she had her laptop, and wifi, so she didn't need much else. Her only imprint was the many plants and flowers that sprung from the corners and shelves, scenting the air with heavy perfumes and clean oxygen.

She'd come a long way from her majestic home amidst the rolling hills of upstate New York, where attending glamorous parties and social networking had been her main function for the business. She'd let Devon, her ex-fiancé, take the reins of her responsibility. Her opinions on running the winery were brushed aside, along with her numerous attempts to expand into catering events and renovate the tasting barn. How many times had he smiled charmingly and told her to let him and her father take care of things? That his future wife shouldn't have to worry about the business that held her name? Even worse, when had it become so easy to step back and let Devon lead? Her father had raised her to be strong, especially after her mother died when she was only twelve years old, but she'd lost her way. His duplicity had forced her to examine what she really wanted out of life, and her own role in this world. She was still figuring it out, but had learned more about herself this past year than her entire overprotected youth.

She glanced at her slim rose gold watch. It was Friday evening and she needed to get out of the house. She might have created a love spell, but chances were slim that her Mr. Right would be knocking at her door. To meet him, she'd have to actually leave the house.

God helps those who help themselves.

She hoped God wasn't too pissed she was relying on a bit of old fashioned witchcraft to find a mate. Anyway, she'd tried church socials numerous times and that certainly wasn't working either. It was harder than she thought to meet interesting, single men and she wasn't the type to be picked up at a bar.

Holding back a sigh, she freshened up, glancing down at her casual, yet sleek outfit of black pants, a snug red shirt, and Prada high-heeled sandals. Her light blond hair was pulled back in a sleek ponytail, and she'd pumped up the volume by adding lots of jewelry. Good enough.

Someone knocked on her door.

Cat froze, staring at the door in a moment of sheer shock and confusion. Could it be? Could the spell have worked that fast? Had her Mr. Right come to her after all—ready to sweep her off her feet?

Her thoughts spun, but she pushed them back and peered through the peephole.

Red petals met her view. "Who is it?" she called out suspiciously.

A feminine voice drifted past the barrier. "Flower delivery for Ms. Winsor."

Relieved and feeling immensely foolish, she swore not to watch *Paranormal Investigations* ever again and opened the door. The bouquet of stunning blood-red roses sprang at her with wild abandon. The delivery person transferred the bouquet, had her scribble her name on a piece of paper, and in moments, she was alone again in her apartment.

Who had sent them? It wasn't her birthday, and she wasn't dating anyone. Hell, she didn't even know many men past the casual acquaintance stage. Excited, she plucked the card from the plastic holder and opened it.

Presto.

A shiver of warning crept down her spine. Suddenly, she was struck by the knowledge something big was about to unfurl—something that would change her life. The dark red petals seemed like an omen of doom rather than a symbol of love and affection. Uneasiness prickled her nerve endings.

What was going on?

Cat frowned, reading the word again. *Soon*. What did this mean? Who would send her red roses with such a cryptic message? She searched for further information but there was nothing else. She tapped the card against her lips and studied the blooms before her. Okay, no need to freak out. She'd just call the flower shop.

It took her only a few minutes to find out the shop knew nothing more. The order had been taken in cash, and the counter person only related he was a tall man with a hoodie pulled over his head. They couldn't tell her any other details.

Cat glanced at the purple fabric-covered book lying on the table.

Yep, she was now freaking out. Best thing to do was get out of her apartment and grab a cocktail. She suddenly needed to be around a noisy, chattering crowd to calm her worries.

She hit the streets, savoring the muggy air, loud city sounds, and bustling shops along the crowded, crooked pavements. Milan reminded her of the energy and style of Manhattan, just with even better architecture. She passed the Moscova Metro station, deciding to take the short walk and head toward *Bar Brera*. April held the hints of summer about to bloom, and ended the quiet season where most Italians and tourists stayed locked up through the crazy high and lows of weather that held no rationale. Today, it was as if the world had woken up and decided to go out for a cappuccino or aperitif to enjoy a mild Friday evening.

When she reached the popular café, all the outdoor tables were already taken. She headed straight toward her favorite bartender—Luigi, who always greeted her in a loud booming voice, flirted shamelessly, and shared pictures of his grandbabies with pride. Living in Italy for the past year had done amazing things for her ego and femininity. She enjoyed the open pleasure men found with women, yet there was a formal respect from the majority that made her feel admired, yet safe. Respected in an old-fashioned sort of way that had been a salve to her soul after being brutally treated.

Of course, she'd occasionally slapped down overeager admirers who mistakenly believed her body was public property. But she viewed the encounters as an opportunity to keep up her defenses. Plus, her right hook.

"*Ciao, bella!*" Luigi called out, recognizing her immediately in the swarming crowd. He plucked the bottle of the Pinot Grigio she preferred, poured a full glass, and adeptly slid it across the bar without pause. *"Come stai?"*

"Bene, bene."

She slid her euros on the bar and took a sip of the chilled liquid. Her gaze surveyed the café, where food and cocktails were being served to the after-work crowd. Three men in sharp suits took up the corner of the bar, staring at her with a tad of lust and little true interest. Holding back a sigh, she looked around for a lone table to enjoy her drink, check her phone, and do some serious people watching.

On her second sweep of the room, she spotted him.

Left corner. No plates on the checkered tablecloth. A bottle of whiskey sat by his right elbow. A heavily cut rocks glass was half filled with the amber liquid, placed perfectly in the center of a square white napkin. The man radiated a dark, brooding type aura that kept the chattering crowd at a distance. As Cat studied him in fascination, she noticed he had rough, jagged lines to his features—from his Roman nose to his heavy black brows and stubbled chin. His cheekbones were two sharp slashes across his face. His lips held a perpetual sneer, tilted down at the sides as if he was a man hard to please. Coal-black hair brushed the top of his ears and was worn too long to be fashionable. His skin was a deep olive. He wore a tight black T-shirt and black pants, casting him in perpetual shadow.

No wonder she hadn't seen him at first. It was as if he was an expert at blending into the background. He was staring into his glass as if it held all the answers, and she held her breath, senses tingling, as she waited for him to look up.

He did.

Lava bubbled through her veins. Her skin flushed at the power of his deep, dark stare, pinning her with eyes as black as obsidian, seething with undertones of sensuality, purpose, and a hint of danger. He held her stare for a few timeless, motionless moments that stretched from seconds to infinity.

Then he looked back down. Lifted his glass. And tipped the liquid down his throat in one long swallow. She watched the muscles of his neck tighten and relax, feeling as if a strange spell had been cast around them both. He slammed the glass down, refilled, and tapped his fingers against the cut rim, as if waiting for something big to happen.

Caterina knew this was a man who was out of her league. She'd usually turn away and seek out a table in the light—where chatter and laughter and light-hearted conversation beckoned. Instead, the memory of the mysterious flowers and the love spell stirred something deep inside. An urge to move forward and push boundaries. An instinct to take a leap and talk with the mysterious stranger.

Her fingers tightened around the stem of her wine glass. She hesitated only a few precious seconds.

Then she walked over to his table.

Chapter Two

He hadn't expected her to notice him.

For the past two days, Rip had gotten the lay of the land and noted where she lived. Her apartment was located in the expensive part of Brera. She wore designer clothes and carried expensive purses and wore glitzy jewelry, even in the afternoon. She walked like a high society woman who'd never been forced to make her own way in life, blinders firmly on, the typical rich white woman who led a cushy, protected life. She had no real job, no regular schedule, and basically did whatever she pleased.

The woman had no grit.

The first time something difficult had slammed her, she'd folded. Left her father and the business and took off to hide in Italy. While Winsor Winery struggled financially, and he and Edward had worked tirelessly to turn a profit, she'd traveled Europe for a year without a job or a care in the world.

This was the woman he had to marry.

Distaste shuddered through him. She was everything he disrespected in the opposite sex—a female with no heart, courage, or honesty. A selfish, silly socialite who worried about no one but herself.

He realized immediately in order to get her attention, he needed to intrigue her. Get her off balance and interested. The roses were just a way to taunt her a bit. He figured she'd go crazy trying to find her secret admirer, and the note was his own private joke. Edward had given him a few hints at her usual routine. Her favorite place to stop in for a drink in the evenings was *Bar Brera*. She haunted a popular pastry shop called *La Dolce Famiglia*. And her favorite spot for relaxation was the *Parco*

Sempione—a park situated behind the tourist attraction *Castillo Sforzesco*. Tonight, he figured he'd make his move and take a chance on the bar.

He'd gotten lucky. He hoped he'd be able to engage her within the first few seconds, and somehow, charm her. There hadn't been a woman in his life who knew about his dark side, or would be able to handle it, but he'd gotten used to hiding the roughness beneath a more appealing exterior. The memory of the woman who'd betrayed him flashed in his mind—of her sweet words and smile that had been just manipulative lies. It'd been so much easier to embrace the numbness afterward. So much easier than messy emotion and raw pain.

So much easier to accept he wasn't meant to be a man who was loved.

He shoved the thoughts from his mind. Caterina Victoria Winsor was like all the other women he'd met, but he needed her. He'd offer plenty of money, social functions, and travel to keep her occupied, in exchange for marrying him and returning home. It would be a marriage in name only—one with little interaction between husband and wife. He would make it work.

Steeling his shoulders, he watched her approach. His gaze collided with a pair of golden eyes, the color of the burning liquid in his rocks glass.

Cat's eyes.

Heat pulsed through his blood with a slow, heavy rhythm that made him clench his hand involuntarily around the bottle. He felt the old emotions explode deep inside, a primitive mixture of raw energy: rage, pain, desire. As he clawed back the dark, swirling mess that fought to surface, Rip realized this woman could be more trouble than he'd originally thought.

His gaze ruthlessly swept her figure. The pictures on Edward's desk didn't do her justice. Blond hair was pulled back from her face. Shoulder length, medium thickness, nothing unusually striking to cause such an odd physical response. Of course, the color wasn't just blond, but ranged from a warm honey brown to the palest of champagne. Her mouth was too wide, her cheeks too plump, and her jaw too angular. Those golden eyes seemed huge in her face, way out of proportion to the rest of her features. Of course, her lips were lush and pale pink, with just a touch of shiny gloss to tempt. Her body had killer curves, emphasized by her tailored black trousers and tight fire engine red shirt.

He pegged her at five feet six inches without those ridiculous four-inch designer shoes.

No, she wasn't his usual type. He preferred brunettes with red lips and no princess attitude. He liked jeans and sneakers and a bawdy sense of humor in his women.

But he hadn't counted on the explosive sexual chemistry that rocked through him. She walked forward with a clear intention etched on her face and a small, sexy smile on her lush lips. Those generous hips swayed as she teetered on her stilettos, clutching her glass in protection, and stopped by his table.

"It won't banish the demons."

Her voice poured over him like thick, sticky honey. The scent of decadence rose to his nostrils: chocolate, musk, and a hint of spice. Seizing on the opportunity, he regarded her with interest. "Are you looking to gain your wings?"

She laughed, a low, husky sound that made his gut clench. "No. I'm sorry I don't have the power to show you what your life could be like." She glanced at the half-filled bottle. "But I do know this stuff is a trap. The demons will still be there, even after the liquid is gone."

He dropped his gaze to hide his shock. This woman was concerned about a stranger in a bar who seemed to be drowning his sorrows in alcohol. Odd, how her concern touched something deep inside him he'd thought dead and buried. He shook off the disturbing feelings and motioned toward her glass. "I doubt white wine could banish even a tiny demon."

Her lips curved in an easy smile. "You're right. I'm probably not one to set a good example. May I join you?"

"Of course."

She slid into the chair opposite him and placed her glass down carefully. The waitress glided over for their order, but he shook his head. Caterina also declined.

"Are you on vacation?"

This was a golden opportunity he refused to miss. Rip knew he had to be careful of how much he revealed. "No. I'm here on business. I'm researching a new project."

She nodded, but didn't pry, and he didn't offer. "We're heading into tourist season."

"You live here?"

"Only temporarily. Been here about a year and a half. Every time I decide to return home, I delay my trip."

Interesting. He shifted in the chair and studied her. "Did you run away from home?"

Her laugh bubbled up from her chest. At least her laugh was real and not that fake giggle he despised. "I guess I did."

"Running from your own demons?"

She took a sip of wine, but her eyes danced with amusement. "You're sharp. Mr—?"

He hesitated, then gave her only his middle name. "No Mister. Just Lee."

She stuck out her hand as if conducting a business meeting. Her skin had a warm, pinkish tone, her fingers long and tapered. Cursing his hesitation, he took her hand and shook. Immediately, his palm prickled from the surge of warmth, and he watched while her eyes widened slightly, obviously experiencing the same jolt. Satisfaction surged. At least it wasn't just him. "Caterina Winsor. Most people call me Cat."

"Caterina." Her name danced on his tongue. He caught the low catch of her breath and something primitive uncurled inside him. "Did running away help?"

Curiosity stirred. What would she tell a stranger about her past? How easy was it for her to lie? She wet her lips in a telltale nervous gesture, and he waited for her to change the subject to safer territory.

"It helped me," she said simply. "If I'd stayed, I would've ended up trying to bury the pain by pretending. Pretending to be okay, pretending not to care that my heart was ripped up. I didn't know who I really was. So I left, even though it hurt some people I love." She seemed to take a fortifying breath, as if reminding herself to be strong. "I needed to figure stuff out, and I did."

"Like what?"

This time, she laughed off his question, probably realizing she'd already gone too deep. "I found I have a passion for good pastries and eat them on a regular basis. I discovered I'd been avoiding carbs for all the wrong reasons, and don't give a crap if I'm overweight because I'm happier eating pasta and bread. I love designing purses and being creative. I adore good leather shoes that cost a fortune and despise espresso and grappa. Is that what you were asking?"

A rare smile curved his lips. She wasn't at all what he'd expected. "What about love?"

She sipped her wine and regarded him with a tilted head. "That's a personal question," she said slowly.

"Isn't that what we're doing?" He lifted his hands and shrugged. "Spilling secrets with strangers in an overcrowded bar?"

"What about you?" she challenged. "What are you trying to drink away?"

Nothing he had any intention of sharing with her. God knows, Rip tried not to think about those days he'd left behind, though the memories still haunted his dreams. "The consequences of my choices," he said.

She frowned. He had the strangest urge to lean over the table and smooth his fingers over the furrow in her brow. "Are you running from them, too?"

He looked deep into her eyes and told the truth. "No. I'm running toward them."

She broke eye contact, but not before he caught the flare of wildness in her golden eyes, the dilation of her pupils, the tiny shudder that wracked her body. He could sense her attraction. Good. It would make things so much easier.

Silence fell between them. She sipped her wine. He drank his whiskey. They shared a comfortable pause. He liked that she seemed content with quiet, didn't feel the need to fill it with idle chatter. A quality so rare in the women of his acquaintance. One that he admired greatly.

"Where are you staying?" she asked.

"At the Grande Hotel."

"Fancy. Your company must be generous."

"It is. And do you live close?"

"Yes, right here in Brera. I love this location. I can hop on the metro, but everything's in walking distance. There are so many wonderful restaurants. Have you eaten dinner?"

"No."

He didn't offer her anything further, wanting her to make the next move.

She paused. He waited, his gaze on her, willing the invitation to spill from her lips. But no invitation came.

Instead, after a brief hesitation, she smiled and lifted her empty glass. "Well, I highly recommend *Ristorante Santa Virginia*. It was nice to meet you, and I hope you have a lovely stay."

He blinked, watching as she unfolded herself from the chair and turned. No. He would not let her leave, not without taking full advantage of their chance meeting to begin his pursuit. Edward hadn't given him much time. "Caterina?"

"Yes?"

"Would you like to join me for dinner?" Those pale pink lips pursed, as if torn by her decision. He upped the stakes. "You were right. I was trying to drown some demons. But after meeting you, I'd rather drive them off with a meal and some conversation." He gave her a sheepish look and ducked his head. "But of course, only if you have time. I'm sure you have better things to do than entertain some stranger on a Friday evening."

His heart pounded, hoping he'd seemed vulnerable enough to intrigue her.

Unbelievably, she gazed at him with unexpected compassion, and sat back down. "I would love to share a meal with you."

He grinned, letting his breath release, and motioned for the waitress. "By the way, I agree wholeheartedly with one of the lessons you learned here in Italy."

"What's that?" she asked.

"Carbs. There's something sexy as hell about watching a woman eat a piece of bread."

A bubbly laugh burst from her lips. "I think we're going to get along just fine."

He thought so, too. Which came as a huge, very welcome surprise. Maybe a marriage between them would be better than he imagined.

Chapter Three

She'd come so close to walking away.

Cat finished her meal and leaned back in her chair to aid digestion. When she'd asked him about dinner, she'd had no intention of actually sharing a meal with him. But he'd seemed so...haunted. Vulnerable. This man intrigued her. He gave off a moody, distant vibe, but when he spoke to her, there was an energy that pulled her in and urged her to linger and look deeper. She craved to know more about him, and over dinner, he'd been the perfect companion. Besides his sharp wit, he was a good listener, holding eye contact and asking pointed questions about her lifestyle.

So far, it had been the best date she'd ever had.

He groaned and duplicated her movement. "I'm stuffed. Even if they came over and put the most perfect cannoli on this table, I'd have to say no."

"Then we're going to need to walk it off," she announced. "Because I'm not letting you leave tonight without taking you to the best dessert place on Earth."

His eyes widened. "You talk a big game, Ms. Winsor. You can't bluff with so much at stake."

She preened with satisfaction. "Trust me, I don't bluff when it comes to pastries. I've been going there regularly for months, and it's become an almost religious experience."

His gaze narrowed with intensity. "Now you're just turning me on."

She laughed, but her cheeks flushed. She ducked her head and rummaged around in her purse. "We need a brisk walk first. Oh, unless you have to leave? I'm sorry, I didn't even check with you."

"No, I don't have to leave," he said softly. His smooth, velvet voice shot tingles down her spine. "What are you doing?"

"Oh, here's my half of the bill." She shoved some euros across the table, but his fierce frown stopped her.

"This is my treat," he said. "You were my honored guest, and I appreciate your company."

Pleasure swamped her. She nodded and put the money back in her wallet. "Then I'll just say *grazie*."

"*Prego.*"

Her thighs tightened. His gaze seemed to delve deep into her soul and find all the hidden, empty spaces inside. Her body whipped to life, and her core softened, growing hot and damp. She hadn't experienced this type of chemistry in so long she wasn't sure what to do about it. She pulled her gaze from his, catching the glint of amusement dancing in those onyx eyes, and rose from the chair. He paid the bill and walked her out.

The night was ripe with earthy scents and the soft glow of moonlight spilling from the dark sky. They fell into an easy stride, walking down the narrowed cobblestone paths, the beautiful lilt of Italian voices mingling in the air. "You never told me what your actual job is," she said. He stiffened beside her, as if he didn't want to answer the question. "I'm sorry, you don't have to tell me. I'm just curious."

"No, it's okay. I'm here to do some research on an acquisition. I just can't discuss details."

She nodded. "I get it. Maybe regarding a property opportunity? It's harder than people think to just visit Milan for a week and get everything done. Americans are so demanding about wanting things completed yesterday."

"Are you full American? Or is there some Italian blood lurking?"

"English, with some Scottish and French. Yet I feel as if I belong here in Italy. This country speaks to me. When I began my travel, I planned on visiting several places to get the full European experience, yet once I arrived here, I never left."

"But you're from New York, correct? I can hear your accent."

"Yes. You, too?"

"How did you know?" he asked.

"One Easterner can recognize another. Say coffee."

He laughed. "Coffee."

"Yep, definitely a New Yorker. We say it like cawfee. I get made fun of all the time."

"It could be worse. I could be a Red Sox fan and talk like a Bostonian."

"Ouch. Sorry, Mets fan here. But I'd prefer Boston over the Yankees any day."

"I guess this is the end of a beautiful friendship."

She couldn't help it. She actually giggled, which wasn't like her at all, but it just spilled out from her mouth before she could stop it. He stared at her, a big grin on his face, and the energy hummed and danced around them, encircling them in a tight hug. Their arms swung close together, fingers barely brushing. Like a schoolgirl, her breath came out in a puffy rush, her skin prickling with awareness at the almost touch.

"Do you plan on going back home?" he asked quietly.

"I did. Time began slipping by faster than I expected. I have to make a decision if I'm going back to my old life, or if I've outgrown it."

He seemed to consider her words. "Maybe you can go back but be different. Maybe it's not about the location, but how you've changed inside."

"Maybe you're right. Here we are."

The storefront sign was done in bold, bright red: *La Dolce Famiglia*. The window of the shop was better than a toy store. The display was lined with bright sunflowers, and endless displays of various pastries seduced onlookers—dusted with powdered sugar, shells crisp and firm, flaky with butter and rich with homemade creams. The little bell tinkled as they walked in. The scent of baked bread, rich chocolate, tangy lemon, and sweet sugar wafted in the air. Even at this late hour, the place was crowded, lines jamming the counters, and the back filled with chattering groups and families sipping cappuccino and snacking on pastries at high round tables.

"Here, I'll take you around first before we get in line so you can decide."

He turned to her, eyes wide. "I may never get out of here alive."

She smiled with agreement. "That's why I can't seem to move out of Milan. Come on."

She led him past the cases, joining him to kneel so they didn't miss the bottom rows of treats. From the *torto al chocolato* that held a touch of wetness from the decadent richness of chocolate, to the fresh fruit *tartlettes* lined up like mini soldiers with strawberries, blueberries, and lemon, to the boxes of firm, moist *ricciarelli*—the delicate almond cookies covered in powdered sugar, the choices were vast and the decision difficult. Cat watched him carefully. His dessert would tell her more about his personality than a dozen pointed questions.

"Are you ready?" she asked.

He cocked his head. "Why do I feel like I'm about to take a test?"

Damn, he was sharp. It was as if he easily guessed all her inner thoughts. She laughed and waved her hand in dismissal. "Not a test. Just curious."

"Why?"

"Desserts tell a lot about a person."

His brows shot up. Suddenly, he leaned in, closing the distance between them. She took in the roughness of stubble hugging his square jaw, the bold slash of his nose, the high arch of his forehead, the liquid blackness of his pupils that hypnotized and pulled her in. His spicy, masculine scent danced in her nostrils. She sucked in a breath at the raw intimacy within those precious few seconds. Those carved lips quirked slightly at the left corner and her belly dropped. "I'll take that challenge. Let's do this."

With an arrogant grin, he tugged her gently into the line. When it was their turn, he pointed directly to the pastry of his choice.

Ah, the *sfogliatelle.*

She'd pegged him for the chocolate torte, but that had been too direct. Her second choice was the *canoli*, but she admitted it was too simple for him. The intricacy of his choice pleased her. Her mind analyzed all the options and sifted through in her usual favorite game. She loved trying to figure out people by their food or drink choice. Wine, especially, since she was a vintner's daughter, but since Milan, she had switched her skills to dessert.

"And you, Caterina? What's your choice?"

She shook herself out of the trance and smiled. "The *panforte,* please. That one." She picked out the slice crammed with hazelnuts, already salivating over the dense, spicy treat. "*Grazie.*"

They took their wrapped snacks on plates and found a table, settling into the stools. Neither of them moved to eat at first. Instead, they took in the perfection of the pastries, enjoying the visual stimuli and taking a deep breath of the rich mix of flavors.

"I had you pegged for the chocolate tart," he said.

She burst into laughter. "I had you pegged as one, too! And I'm not wrong often."

"I guess both of us have secrets." His stark words made her shiver, as if he gave her a warning. Her tummy clenched and she crossed her legs, trying to ignore the quick surge of heat that seemed to burst between them in regular intervals. Who would've thought she'd meet a man in a local bar and have it turn into the longest, most perfect date she'd ever experienced?

She forked up a piece of her treasure, closing her eyes as she enjoyed the explosion of dense bread, spicy nuts, sweet fruits, and the mix of gorgeous honey coating her tongue.

He cleared his throat and shifted on his stool. She fought a blush as she realized her moan had made him a bit uncomfortable. "*Mi dispiace.*"

Humor lit his gaze. "No need to be sorry for enjoying your dessert." He cut off a piece of his pastry, exposing the semi-sweet, heavy ricotta cheese baked into layers of thin, crispy dough and smothered with powdered sugar. "Now, tell me what my *sfogliatelle* tells you about me."

She tapped the fork against her mouth. "Well, you have layers."

He snorted. "We all have layers."

She tossed him a mock glare. "Are you going to argue right away with my insights or let me finish?"

His lip twitched. "Go ahead."

"As I was saying, you have layers. Some are easier to figure out than others. You put out a neutral, cool type of distance and don't like to get to really know people. You don't trust easily and prefer to depend only on yourself." Ah, that got his attention. He stared at her with a hint of caution, as if she'd really surprised him. Cat warmed up to the game, excited she seemed to be on the right track. "But inside, there's a sweetness, a vulnerability. You hate tapping into it, because it reminds you of something in your past that changed you. You're much more complicated than you let on."

He paused mid-bite, a deep frown creasing his brow. A strange energy whipped around him, a primitive type of male force that fascinated her, but he quickly got it under control and he was back to normal in seconds. An easy grin curved his lips. "Do you read tea leaves, too?"

"Nope. I dislike tea."

"Along with grappa and espresso. Good to know." He swallowed another bite, his tongue swiping off the sugar, and suddenly her blood steamed like hot lava and she had a crazy urge to lean across the table and kiss him. What would his full lips feel like against hers? Were his muscles as hard as they looked? Would he kiss her with a hint of violence, or surprise her with a stirring type of sweetness, like his dessert? "Ready for my analysis now?"

She swallowed and re-focused. "Sure."

"The *panforte* is the traditional fruit cake that Americans usually mock for being bland, cheap, and too heavy. But the Italians have managed to master it to an art form, which is a quest for specific flavors to balance and play off each other in the ultimate taste."

His words dripped with sensuality. His voice deepened and his gaze pinned her across the table, weaving a spell. Her heart pounded and her palms dampened. She tried to speak, but found her mouth too dry.

He lifted his fork. "May I?" he asked.

Still silent, she managed to nod. He broke off a piece, placing it on his tongue, then closed his eyes as he registered the flavors.

Cat swayed in her chair and realized she now knew exactly what it was like to swoon. Holy crap, he was seducing her with her own game and he didn't even know it. Or maybe he did.

His eyes opened. "Ah, it's a trick. At first, all the complicated textures and tastes can throw a person off and make them believe you're a bundle of contradictions. Normally, this type of dessert would peg you as challenging, assertive, and a complete emotional mess."

Her jaw dropped. "You got all that?"

"I'm not finished. The *panforte* is a trick. Because the goal of the dessert is to balance all that chaos into one perfect experience. This slice features ripe figs, a touch of orange peel, chocolate, hazelnuts, and is that clove? Coriander? Something to add spice. It's a jumble, but somehow, it works to achieve one lasting note. Which means you're actually quite stable. Quietly intelligent and not as flashy as people believe you are. In that way, you put on your own show and don't allow too many people to see the real you. Yet your feelings run deep, and there's something you're craving. Something you haven't found, something you're still searching for with a kind of desperation."

"And what do you think that something is?"

His gaze dropped to her mouth. The word dropped from his lips like a gunshot.

"Passion."

Oh, my God. How could he possibly know that? Heat slithered in her veins, between her legs, tingling her breasts. Breathless, she held his gaze and waited. Seconds ticked by. What would happen next? What did she want to happen?

"Caterina! *Ciao!*"

The warm voice cut through their connection and put an end to the intense standoff. She turned, strangely relieved, her mouth breaking into a huge smile at the familiar figure. Rising from her chair, she stepped over and hugged the older woman, who wrapped her in strong arms and returned her embrace with full enthusiasm. "Mama Conte, I'm so glad I didn't miss you. You're working late."

The matriarch of the pastry empire, *La Dolce Famiglia*, was a familiar presence in the Milan bakery. With her long grey hair twisted up in a bun, her features were classic and elegant, hinting at a shimmering beauty from youth. Generous laugh lines were carved into her olive skin. She wore wide-legged black pants and a simple white blouse on her petite frame. She suffered from arthritis and walked with a cane, but as the mother of four children and a powerful force in the food empire and business world, she cut a dynamic figure. From the first day Cat had stumbled into the bakery, Mama Conte had treated her with a nurturing warmth she desperately needed, until her regular visits were not only about the treats, but the company. The Conte family made her feel alive and welcome, and reminded her of her father, soothing some of the sting from missing him.

Her sharp brown gaze took in her companion, and she blew off Cat's question with a generous smile and a humph. "Michael gives me a hard time but sometimes I crave being in the store. Talking to people was a critical part of our success. No one likes to eat good dessert alone. You need good conversation. Good company, *sì*? Especially from handsome young men. Who is this, my child?"

"Oh, yes, this is Lee. I told him he had to experience the power of *La Dolce Famiglia*."

Lee smiled warmly and shook her hand. "Signora Conte, a pleasure to meet you. Your bakery is extraordinary."

"*Grazie*. Everyone calls me Mama Conte. I'm glad Caterina was able to share her love for a well baked dessert." Her dark eyes held a mysterious glint. "Are you staying with us for a while, I hope?"

"A week. I'm here for work, but I was lucky enough to be saved from a lonely dinner tonight."

Cat tried not to blush, but Mama Conte looked delighted. "*Perfecto*. Why don't you both come to dinner Sunday afternoon? You both need a good home cooked meal. Too much fast food at cafés ruin the stomach."

Her eyes widened. "Oh, that's so nice of you but we just met, and I don't think—"

"You must come. One o'clock. I shall make you a special dessert."

She glanced at Lee in embarrassment. Oh, my God, what if he had no interest in seeing her again? What if he was involved with someone else? She'd seen no ring but nowadays a woman never knew. Trying not to panic, she began to stammer like she always did when she got nervous. "Umm, Mama Conte, *grazie*, but Lee has work and I have, well I have—"

"Sundays are meant for pleasure and the Lord, not work." Her booming voice brooked no argument. The woman beamed a smile, scribbled something on one of the business cards in her pocket and handed it to Lee. "You'll need to take the *funicular* to my home in Bergamo, but it's not too far."

"Oh, but you see, I can't because we—"

"We'd love to come." Lee's deep voice interrupted her pathetic attempts to reject the invitation. Her head swiveled around to stop him, to tell him he didn't have to, but Mama Conte was already nodding with satisfaction.

"*Bene*! I must go, or Michael will worry." She hugged and kissed her, then Lee, and walked out of her bakery with her head held high and a smooth grace, even with her slight limp.

"Caterina?"

She jerked around. "Yes?"

"Breathe. I think you're freaking out."

She half closed her eyes and groaned. "I'm so sorry, Lee. I didn't know she was going to bully you into dinner with me. Listen, forget the whole thing. I'm going to tell her I got sick and you had to work, it's absolutely no problem."

A frown touched his brow. "Well, that would be a problem to me. Because I want to go to dinner with you and experience a real homemade meal at Mama Conte's house."

She blinked. "You do?"

"Of course. It's a win-win. I get to spend more time with you, and I get to eat. Unless you don't want to go with me?"

Her worries scattered away and left her with a sense of budding excitement. Her nerves tingled. "I do."

He grinned. "Good. Then let's finish up so I can walk you home."

They ate their desserts and walked side by side. Crowds had thinned. Shops closed up. The click of her heels on the pavement and their whispered voices added a sense of intimacy to the stroll. He stopped outside her place.

"Thank you for a perfect evening," he said.

"Thank you."

He studied her in the darkness. His gaze drifted over her face, similar to a caress, and then he smiled. "*Buona sera*, Caterina."

Tongue tied and ridiculously hoping for a kiss, she said her goodbye and dove for the door. Peeking out the window, she watched him pivot on his heel and disappear down the road. Feeling as if her head were stuffed with cotton balls, she drifted up the steps and walked inside. The scent of ripe roses hung heavy in the air.

She threw her purse on the table and stood in front of the flowers. Her fingers touched a velvet petal, and a shiver shot down her spine.

Presto.

Soon.

Who sent them? Did she have a secret admirer who'd been keeping his distance, afraid to approach? Normally, the thought would thrill her, but tonight, a strange uneasiness bubbled through her veins. Tonight had been special. For the first time, she'd met a man who intrigued her, and she didn't want to break the spell by thinking of another unknown man lurking in the background.

The spell....

She gasped, her gaze falling on the violet-covered book.

Impossible. Just a coincidence. Right?

She thought of her list hidden under her mattress and shivered. She was on overload, and there was too much to think about right now. She'd get into her comfy pajamas, crawl into bed, and get some sleep.

Tonight, she would dream of seething dark eyes, rich *panforte*, and soul-stirring, carnal kisses.

Tomorrow, she would ponder the mystery of the flowers.

Chapter Four

Rip took in the sprawling terra cotta villa perched on the peak of a hill. The walled city of Bergamo was snugly situated at the foothills of the Alps and separated into upper and lower towns. The combination of old and new mingled into sheer perfection, leaving the bustling city of Milan a distant memory.

Mama Conte's estate included a sloping roof, wrought iron balconies, and elaborate stone pillars flanking the front door. Bright yellow and red surfaces competed with bursting buds of wildflowers in vivid colors. The massive white-peaked tips of the Alps shimmered in the distance.

He turned toward Caterina, taking in the slight nervousness of her features, and found his heart softening. She wore a floral dress in sunny yellow, leaving her hair to spill loosely over her shoulders. A gold chain with a heart locket circled her neck. Her makeup was light and natural, allowing him to catch the beauty mark on her right cheek, and the warm pinkish glow to her skin. She looked different today—more approachable and down-to-earth, though her shoes were low-heeled Louboutins and completely impractical for walking. But she'd warned him about her passion for shoes, and kept her complaints to a minimum as she picked her way through the cobblestones and trekked up the hill toward the *funicular*—the cable railway that pulled them up the steep hill from Milan to Bergamo. The moment he greeted her, her cheeks flushed and her amber eyes glowed with open pleasure. She was genuinely happy to see him, and not even trying to hide it, which made an answering leap of his heart he tried to ignore.

He should be thrilled his plan was going so well. Their date had been flawless. Even better, she'd made the first move, approaching him, not the other way around. But her unexpected warmth and openness, the way she had him yearning for more, made his gut twist with tension.

And guilt.

Since his conversation with Edward, he'd never once considered they could have a real, intimate relationship. Yet, he'd spent the last two days thinking about her, and nights dreaming of her naked and in his bed, until he woke in a tangle of sheets with a throbbing erection and an ache in his chest.

The game had turned on him. For the first time in years, he actually craved a woman's touch. She wasn't supposed to be funny and sweet. She was supposed to be a shallow, spoiled socialite who cared nothing about anyone else.

"Are you ready?" he asked, shifting the bottle of Chianti and bouquet of fresh flowers they'd brought for their hostess.

"Yes, it'll be fun."

He knocked on the door, and it was answered by a lovely young woman who immediately ducked her head with shyness, offering a smile from beneath the mass of dark curls sliding over her cheek. "*Buon Giorno*! Come in. I'm Carina."

He stepped inside, and the scents of garlic, lemon, and basil assaulted his senses. "Nice to meet you, Carina. I'm Lee, and this is Cat. Thank you so much for having us."

A rapid rush of Italian rose in the air. Carina sighed and shouted back. "I got the door, Mama, and I'm bringing them into the kitchen! Sorry, Mama's cooking, follow me."

The girl led them down the short hallway and paused in the archway of the long, open kitchen. Ceramic tile gleamed clean and bright and set off the pine cabinets and heavy table. Massive counters flanked the room and were covered with fresh herbs, tomatoes, and an array of pots and pans.

Two women stepped before them—a dual vision of thick black hair, strong features, and dark eyes. They looked similar to Carina but older, and more confident. Closing the distance, they gave them warm hugs, making Rip feel like an old family friend.

"Welcome to our home," the shorter, curvier brunette said. "My name is Venezia."

"I'm Julietta," the taller woman said. Her husky voice held an undertone of authority. She wore a conservative business suit, and her smile held the practiced ease of someone comfortable in a leadership role. Rip pegged her for early thirties.

Venezia motioned toward the man setting out bottles of wine on the counter, and he walked over. "And this is my boyfriend, Dominick." The man nodded and shook their hands, his brown eyes and curly dark hair cutting a striking appearance. His arm hooked around Venezia's waist with a casual affection that hinted at a long-term relationship, even though there was no ring on Venezia's finger. "Happy to have you," he said.

"Mama has been wanting to invite you to dinner for a long time, Cat. She says you are our best customer," Julietta said.

"I am. Is it wrong to even worry about the extra ten pounds I gained due to her baking skills?"

Venezia waved her hand in the air. "Women with curves are treated like goddesses here in Italia, right, Carina?"

The younger girl smiled, but she shifted under her baggy clothes as if she was still trying to accept her body. Rip thought she looked around twenty, but still in the midst of dealing with physical and emotional changes. Women were always so hard on themselves with looks, especially in an American culture that relished thinness and judged with a vicious ruthlessness anyone different. Rip winked at her. "Personally, I refuse to date a woman who won't eat bread. It's a deal-breaker for me."

Carina laughed.

He handed Julietta the wine and flowers, nodding at her thanks, then eased them into the main kitchen area where the cooking was happening. "Mama treats Sundays like a national holiday in our home. I hope you brought your appetite."

Mama Conte stood in the middle of what looked like chaos. Water bubbled from pots on the stove, and thick loaves of freshly baked bread were laid out on the counters. Chunks of mozzarella cheese, vine ripened tomatoes, and bottles of olive oil were set out on plates. A huge *antipasti* platter filled with meats, olives, roasted red peppers, and more cheese sat next to the bread. A pasta machine held freshly made noodles laid out in straight lines. A large apron with *La Dolce Famiglia* scrolled on the front covered most of her figure. She wiped her floured hands on a red towel, beaming and opening her arms in greeting when she saw them.

"Welcome! Ah, such beautiful flowers, *grazie*." They were enveloped in more hugs, and Rip realized he'd never had so much affection bestowed on him than these past few minutes in the Conte household. "Sit. Dominick, get them a glass of vino, *per favore*. Carina, will Maximus be joining us today with your brother?"

Carina turned beet red. "No, he stayed in Milano today and won't be back till late. He's working."

Mama Conte shook her head. "*Mama mia*, does no one respect a Sunday any longer?" She turned a fierce look toward Julietta. "Do not even think of sneaking out early to go back to the office."

Julietta sighed. "I'm working on a new deal to expand. Michael and I may need to leave early."

"Not when we have company. Venezia, did you make the *ricciarelli* like I asked?"

Venezia groaned. "I told Carina to do it! I've been busy."

"Looking at all those fashion magazines," Carina shot back.

Her sister rolled her eyes. "For inspiration. I have another casting call this week and need to make sure I get it right."

Dominick dropped a kiss on her pouty lips. "You'll be *perfecto*. They will be crazy not to book you for the magazine cover."

Caterina looked fascinated by the frantic chatter back and forth that seemed a trademark to a big family. "Venezia, are you a model?"

"*Sì*. I've done local magazines but I want to be on Italian Vogue one day."

"Aren't you too short?" Julietta asked.

Venezia gasped and threw up her hands. "No! I've gotten plenty of bookings and you're just jealous that you're stuck in an office all day."

Julietta snorted. "I don't think so. I make more money than you."

Another gasp. Carina giggled.

Rip turned his head to hide his growing amusement. He'd always wondered what it would be like to have siblings. He wondered if the bond of blood trumped all the petty arguments. He had an instinct that in the Conte household, love was the real glue that held together their family.

Venezia began yelling in Italian, while Dominick soothed her at the same time as he ate bread and poured glasses of red wine, once again demonstrating to Rip he'd done this with his lover many times.

Mama Conte stamped her foot. "*Basta e basta*! Venezia, put on an apron and get to work. Carina, get the plates out and begin slicing bread. Julietta, call your brother pronto and tell him we are all waiting on him. Dominick, finish your bread at the table. You are trailing crumbs everywhere."

Rip watched as order replaced chaos. Mama Conte smiled at them and winked. "*Mi dispiace*. Venezia and Dominick have been dating for many years. They fight as often as they steal kisses."

"Mama," Venezia groaned. "We are adults yet you still talk of us like children. And we haven't fought once today."

"Stop your bickering with your sister and cook. Now, if we have not scared you away yet, please enjoy the *antipasto*."

Caterina met his gaze, eyes full of humor and a softness that told him she was as comfortable in Mama Conte's kitchen as she'd likely be at one of her high society parties. This new layer revealed there was much more to his future wife than he'd originally thought.

$$* * * *$$

An hour later, they were gathered around the table in the middle of what seemed like the Last Supper. Rip had never seen so much food in his life. After the appetizers, big bowls of pasta with gravy were brought out, accompanied by meatballs, neckbones, and sausage. Then the salad course—greens drizzled with fragrant oils and earthy balsamic. But his jaw dropped when Mama Conte whipped out the *branzino*, the delicious flaky fish so fresh, he wondered if there was a sea behind the villa. Crisp asparagus, stuffed artichokes, sautéed mushrooms, and garlic bread topped with parmigiano were put out almost as an afterthought. The family didn't blink, expertly serving and passing large bowls of food, and re-filling glasses with ruby red Montepulciano that held fragrant undertones of blackberry and currants, with a smooth tannin.

Michael arrived right before the first course, kissing Mama Conte's cheek in apology as she muttered about his workaholic ways. The oldest son emitted a charisma and laid-back energy that had probably made him a force in the business. He had long dark hair tied in a ponytail, and was dressed in a smart Armani jacket, tailored pants, and leather shoes. But his dark eyes danced as he introduced himself as the head of the family, hinting at a wicked sense of humor he revealed when he began teasing Carina about stealing Venezia's modeling jobs because she was the most beautiful.

That brought another enthusiastic round of bickering, underlaid with affection.

For a few seconds, Rip gazed at the scene before him with a pain in his chest, a raw need welling up from inside he'd never given himself permission to feel. He couldn't imagine what it would be like to grow up in this type of household, with an actual family who gave a shit. One who spent Sunday dinners together, arguing and teasing and forgiving, trying to be heard in the midst of boisterous chatter and loudly spoken opinions. A family who also knew the power of silence and when to be quiet and listen, evident by the way Mama Conte regarded her children around the table, occasionally cutting one of them off to make room for another to speak, especially Carina, who was the shyest.

"Mama Conte, tell us how you got into the pastry business," Rip asked, curious about her backstory.

"I was taught how to bake since I was a *bambina*. My mama was always in the kitchen, and Papa worked at a bakery in Milano. It is part of my blood and my heritage. It was my husband who suggested we could open up our own bakery. Michael was just born, and we were struggling as most do when they are young. But I was known for my pastries. The moment I baked a batch, they would disappear and people would ask for more."

"It must have been scary to take everything you have and invest in a new business," Caterina said.

The woman's eyes grew misty with memory. A small smile rested on her lips. "*Sì*. Many nights we'd lie in bed and I'd beg my husband to forget the plan. But he always believed in me. He insisted I baked my treats with a magic potion that made people come back for more. Bergamo had no known pastry shops like in Milano and we wanted to stay close to home. We opened with just a few pastries on the menu. By the next week, I needed to increase my baking because we sold out daily."

Julietta reached out and squeezed her mother's hand. "Papa loved working in the kitchen, but he said Mama was the one with the gift. He headed the business portion, but they always worked as a team."

"When did you lose him?" Rip asked quietly.

"A few years ago. To a heart attack," Venezia said.

"But he is always here with us," Mama Conte said, glancing at the space at the end of the table, where her son now sat. "And now my children have taken the reins and made us both proud."

Julietta smiled. "Mama and Papa taught us young to always go big with dreams as long as you paired it with hard work. Now, Michael and I run the business portion of *La Dolce Famiglia* and we are expanding."

Rip cocked his head. "Where?"

"America. New York," Michael said. He drummed his fingers on the pine table, excitement gleaming in his dark eyes. "I'm in the process of securing our first location in a place called the Hudson Valley. I'll be heading there in the next few weeks."

Cat gasped. "Are you kidding me? My family owns a business in that same area."

Rip stiffened as a surge of anger rushed through him. Family business? She had no right to call it a family business when she was Edward's only family. What did she have to do with the business? Absolutely nothing.

Would she tell them how she ran away and left the winery practically bankrupt? Would she admit to spending her father's money on an expensive hiatus, traveling without a care? He kept his gaze trained on her, studying every expression flickering over her face.

Venezia gasped. "That is amazing. What are the odds? What type of business do you have, Cat?"

"It's called Winsor Winery. We bottle and distribute wine, and do tastings and events. We outsource the bulk of grapes, then blend the wine in house. It's been part of my family for generations and we are one of the oldest wineries in the state."

Anger simmered in his gut. How dare she use the word *we*? No, *he'd* been the one to work night and day, calling in endless contacts, pulling the business back from bankruptcy while she flitted around Europe. His hands clenched the stem of his wineglass and he dragged in a breath.

Michael chuckled. "I will definitely be visiting you and your father."

Mama Conte regarded her thoughtfully. "I did not know you left all this behind. You never spoke about it."

Caterina drew in a breath, glancing around the table at the curious stares. Rip waited for her to swiftly change the subject or give them a breezy answer. Instead, she managed to surprise him.

Again.

"Because it hurt too much," she said. "My ex-fiancé was my father's partner in the business. I found him cheating on me in the cellars. After that, I couldn't visit the winery without remembering." Staring down at her lap, she let out a sigh before sitting up and locking eyes with Mama Conte. "So I left."

A collective murmuring of sympathy rose from the table. Venezia and Julietta shook their head in fierce disapproval.

"That is horrible," Venezia exploded. "Did you kill him first?"

Caterina smiled. "I wanted to, but they frown on things like murder in the US. I decided to travel and figure out why I wanted to stay with a man who didn't love me, let alone respect me. It took me a year and a half, but I've finally figured out who I am apart from my ex, my father, and the winery."

"Your papa must have been devastated," Michael said with a hard glint in his eye. "First, betrayed by a trusted friend. Then to lose his daughter to heartbreak."

"Yes, it was hard for both of us." Suddenly, she glanced over at Rip, and their gazes locked. Her voice trembled slightly. "But I know better now. I know what I deserve. What I want. I won't make such a mistake again."

The energy surged between them, catching heat and exploding like firecrackers. He sucked in a breath and tumbled into those golden eyes that promised him something he'd only dreamed of. For a brief moment, his surroundings fell away, and he was alone with her. She'd told the truth and held nothing back. This couldn't be the woman he first imagined. Should he confess his secret before they fell even further into each other? Or would that be a mistake when his entire future was on the line?

Michael cleared his throat, and Rip jerked back into the moment. He caught their knowing smiles, and Cat dropped her head, trying to hide a blush.

"It is brave to begin anew," Mama Conte said. "But we mustn't allow others to steal our home, or our memories. I am sure your papa would want you home, where you belong."

Her voice came out tight with emotion. "*Grazie*. He is a wonderful man and I know he misses me. It was hard for him to let me go."

"Do you want to go back to the winery?" Julietta asked. "I can't imagine walking away from the family business. It's a part of who I am."

Rip leaned over, intent on her answer.

A sigh escaped her lips. "It's hard to explain. Winsor Winery is part of my heritage but I was never given a choice to do anything else. My entire life revolved around the will of the grapes. I was attending important social functions when I was just a teenager. As much as I treasure those memories, I want to choose my own course. I don't want to go back right now. I'm not ready. I'm sure it's hard to understand."

Rip caught Michael and Mama Conte sharing a meaningful look.

For an instant, there was pain carved out on Michael's face, until it was quickly cleared and Rip wondered if it had just been his imagination.

"I understand better than you know, Cat," Michael said quietly. A hush came over the table as if everyone was processing his answer. "But sometimes we must do what is right for family, even if it takes us on a different path."

Cat nodded. "You're right. I've found happiness in Italy, but if my father needed me, I'd do what had to be done. Family always comes first."

His gaze narrowed. Was she telling Mama Conte what she believed the woman wanted to hear? Or did Caterina truly believe she'd respond to Edward if he needed her? Rip leaned toward her. The question burst from his lips without filter. "Would you?"

She tilted her head and regarded him. "Would I what?"

"Go home if your father asked you?"

Those golden eyes flickered with an array of emotions. He searched deep to discern truth or lie, and waited for her answer. "Yes," she said simply. "If my father needed me, I'd do whatever I had to."

The surge of tenderness took him by surprise. He had to fist both of his hands to stop from reaching for her and pulling her into his embrace, to offer comfort, to stroke her hair and kiss her and tell her it would all be okay. Where had such tenderness come from? Such a haunting need for her touch?

Why had her confession stirred him? She'd been a young girl with a future planned out. How had she felt walking in on her fiancé with another woman? Had she questioned everything she'd once believed in? Had running away been her only option as her life crumbled around her?

Yet, she lived off of her father's money while he struggled to keep his business alive. She spoke of Winsor Winery as part of her heritage, but chose to walk away when her father needed her most. The battle inside him warred, spilling a bunch of messy emotions he wasn't able to sort through.

Then again, did it matter? She'd uttered the words he needed to hear. That she would do what her father asked if needed. Her pledge sealed both of their fates. The marriage would proceed unopposed.

Completely unaware of the importance of the event, Mama Conte and Michael smiled. Julietta raised her glass. "To family."

"To family," they all chimed in. Rip ignored the pain in his gut and drank anyway, then stared at Cat in moody silence.

Why didn't he feel victorious? Was it because he wished he had the time to win her heart on his own, rather than making her feel forced into a marriage with him?

"May I ask you an important question?" Julietta ventured.

Caterina smiled. "Of course."

"Do you think you'd help me with a wine pairing for Mama's pastries? Michael, wouldn't that be a wonderful idea to draw more traffic into the *La Dolce Famiglia* on a weeknight?"

Michael nodded. "*Dio*, it's a brilliant idea. We could offer a special tasting menu. If Caterina would agree, of course."

"I'd be honored to help out," Cat said immediately. "My skills have been rusty so this would be helpful to ease back in."

Venezia sighed with dramatic flair. "Don't you two ever stop working?"

Carina squealed. "Can I help? I love wine pairing."

"You just love your wine," Venezia retorted.

"And you've never wanted to be a part of the bakery," Carina shot back.

"And you've never respected my decision to go into fashion!"

As the sisters argued, Dominick smiled and kissed his lover's palm, and Venezia immediately softened, as if he held a power over her that only she answered to. Once again, an aching need scratched its way to the surface, making Rip wonder how it would feel once Caterina belonged to him.

As his wife.

Afternoon bled into evening. Dinner was replaced with dessert. He drank bitter espresso with the sting of *sambucca* and feasted on *ricciarelli*—the rich, chewy almond cookies bringing a moan to his lips. The *tiramisu* was also a highlight—ladyfingers soaked in brandy, smothered in cream, and topped with dusted chocolate. They ate and talked and laughed until Michael and Julietta finally left, apologizing for departing early and thanking Caterina for her help with the pairings. Venezia followed shortly after, accompanying Dominick to a party, and Carina left to study for an exam.

"We better get going," Caterina sighed, holding his gaze. "This has been the most wonderful evening. If I could just use the bathroom?"

"Of course, down the hall and to the left."

"*Grazie.*"

She left them alone. Rip smiled at Mama Conte. "Thank you for including me in your dinner. It's a night I'll never forget."

"It was a pleasure to have you in my home. Do you have a close family, Lee?"

He jerked at the direct hit. Then tried to recover. "No. I haven't seen my parents since I left for college at nineteen."

"Were they unsupportive? Not understanding? Or was there a bigger reason you don't talk any longer?"

Usually, he'd resent a person prying into his private life, but somehow, with Mama Conte, it felt different. "They were cruel."

He prepared himself for pity, but she only nodded, as if she'd heard many stories in her lifetime. "Hard to have no one to trust in this world," she said. "Still, a man who makes his own way is a powerful force."

The words fell from him with a rare honesty. "I don't need to trust anyone but myself."

Those shrewd, dark eyes glinted with intention. She leaned across the table, startling him when she clasped his hand. Her skin was warm and rough and comforting, the touch of a mother, nurturing and strong at the same time. "Ah, but that is a trap. We all need someone to trust." She paused and squinted, looking deeper into his eyes. "You have many ghosts you are fighting, no?"

Shock kept him silent for a moment. He tried to force a laugh, but his voice got stuck. A strange foreboding rose up from inside him, urging him to tell her the truth. "Yes," he finally said. "But I've got them under control."

Her gaze ripped and shredded the lies away. "You and Cat seem to have a connection."

"Yes," he said again.

She nodded, her fingers squeezing his hard. "Then you will need to fight for her," she said. "Do not be afraid to love. Sometimes it's the only thing that keeps the ghosts away. *Capisce?*"

The strange conversation should have made him pull away, pat her hand, and forget. Instead, his gut clenched and he recognized the truth, a truth he'd been avoiding for a very long time. The truth of why he never pursued or kept himself in relationships or tried to share any part of himself.

Because every time he opened up, he was reminded he didn't matter. Not to his father who consistently reminded him he was trash.

Not to the woman he'd thought he'd loved who'd betrayed him. And not to Edward Winsor. It didn't matter how hard he worked, or how much money he made, or how much success he'd achieved. In the end, he only ended up alone.

The admission ripped from his soul. "I don't know if I can."

She smiled, easing her grip, and patted his hand in comfort. "You are a good man. And you can, Lee. Don't underestimate yourself."

She sat back in her chair the exact moment Caterina walked into the kitchen. "Are you ready?"

His legs shook a bit, but he nodded and stood. "Yes."

They said their goodbyes, promising to stop at the bakery soon, and left.

But Mama Conte's words haunted him.

Chapter Five

Caterina wondered what he was thinking about.

She glanced over and caught the clench of his jaw, the haunted glint in his inky eyes, the tension of his shoulders. Oh, he held up his conversation with ease on the way home from Bergamo, but even in this short time, she sensed he was putting on an act.

"Did Mama Conte say something to you before we left?" she asked. Since the moment they met, their short relationship had been based on truth. She refused to begin playing games at this juncture. Go big or go home, right?

He jerked. She realized they'd stopped once again in front of her door, a déja vu from the first night they met. Tension simmered as they gazed at each other in the darkness on the quiet street. It had rained earlier. The pavement was wet, and a damp muskiness rose in the air. The lazy drip of water from the roof was the only sound. "Why do you ask?"

"Because you're acting different. As if she said something that bothered you."

His lips tightened into a thin line. "No, everything's fine."

Why did his answer piss her off? Just because he didn't want to share what happened? It probably wasn't her business. Yet, the knowledge he didn't want to answer her question nagged and rankled at her confidence. Maybe she was making this thing between them into more than it was. After all, he'd be gone soon, and she'd be...here. Still trying to decide what to do next with her life. Suddenly, her excitement over a possible handbag business seemed to dim. Why was she thinking of her father and the winery? Her thoughts spun and she sought safety in the isolation of her room. She needed to think. "Okay. Thanks for the nice evening."

She turned and put her hand on the knob.

His hand shot out and grabbed her arm. "You're upset. What's the matter?"

Her gaze narrowed. "It's late. We're both tired. I'm just ending the evening politely."

Those fierce brows lowered in a frown. "What if I don't want the evening to end just yet? Why don't you tell me why you're suddenly angry?"

Her temper rose. "Why are you pushing? This is crazy! We met two days ago and spent an entire afternoon with Mama Conte at a family dinner. Who does that? And you've been acting like something's bothering you since we left but you won't tell me what it is. I'm sorry, I need to back off. I need to think."

Suddenly, he leaned in, a magnificent male specimen who practically pulsed with raw emotion. "What are you so afraid of?"

"It's too soon for all...this. I've known you for two days and I'm telling you these things about myself—it's too intimate. It's better if we slow down. Analyze what's happening between us."

"Wrong. I think you're tired of being in your head and trying to make sense of what this is." The spicy, musky scent of his rose to her nostrils and made her crave. "From the moment we met, there's been a connection between us. What I'm feeling for you right now demands intimacy and some risk. Are you trying to deny it?"

Her belly dropped to her toes, and immediately her body softened in response. This was what she wanted. The realness. The sloppy, messy slide of feelings that wrecked logical thought and made her feel alive again.

"No." She closed her eyes, struggling to communicate the fear of being wrong about him. "I-I just don't want this to be a lie. I don't want to believe this is us together and give you stuff only to watch you distance yourself at the end and leave. Oh, God, I sound so stupid and confused, just—tell me the truth. If this is a short affair while you're in town, fine, but I need to know."

His fingers closed over her shoulders and he pushed her gently against the door. She sucked in a breath as she was surrounded by the sheer breadth of his body against hers. He gazed down at her like a dark angel intent on claiming her, his eyes seething with intensity. "Do you want to know what Mama Conte said to me?" he challenged, his face inches from hers. "She told me not to be afraid to love. She said it's the only thing that keeps the ghosts away. And God knows, Caterina, I have plenty of ghosts, and it's a hell of a lot easier to stay away from anyone who threatens my peace, or my heart. But when I look at you, I want things I've never wanted before. How is that for truth?"

She shuddered. Her skin burned for his touch. She lifted her fingers and traced the savage curve to his lips. "I don't know you," she whispered. "It's too much."

"I want you to know me," he grated out. "For the first time in my life, I want to share things with you. Show the hidden parts no one else has seen, and God help me, it scares the living shit out of me."

The truth of his words vibrated in his voice, his gaze, his trembling hands as he cupped her cheeks and pressed his forehead to hers. His breath whispered across her lips.

"Me, too," she whispered.

His velvet rich voice held her spellbound. "Then kiss me so we both don't have to be afraid anymore."

She rose on tiptoes to meet him halfway and then his mouth met hers. She prepared herself for a sensual invasion, but his lips skated gently, teasingly, as if an experiment was being played out. With slow, easy movements his tongue traced the outline of her lips in the lightest of caresses, and with a delicious precision that made a pulsing liquid warmth flow through her body. Almost as if he was afraid she'd bolt any moment, his arms slipped around her waist and eased her closer.

His ruthless control allowed her to relax in his embrace, craving more. With a low murmur of satisfaction, he suddenly drew back. His seething gaze registered her surrender. A moment passed as they stared at one another. Her heart beat wildly in her chest.

Then he bent his head once again, and with one swift motion, re-slanted his mouth over hers. His tongue surged past the seam of her lips in one shocking, heated stroke.

Claimed.

Her body shuddered as Lee possessed her mouth with all the fierce determination of a warrior claiming his woman. His tongue swept through the damp, silken interior, tasting her, seducing her, as each deep, hot stroke told her again and again that she belonged to him.

Her toes curled in her expensive Louboutins as he pressed into the small of her back, cradling her hips against his. She gasped at the bold feel of his arousal, and he swallowed the sound with a greediness that made an answering wave of heat pool between her thighs. Her nails dug into the muscles of his shoulders as she fought for balance, fought the need to match him thrust for thrust, fought the sweet, wild fire pumping through her veins.

"No, Caterina," he breathed against her mouth. His teeth nipped her bottom lip and his voice poured over her like warm honey, darkly commanding. "Don't fight it. Open yourself to me; give me everything you have, sweetheart. Kiss me back. I need it. I need you."

Then his mouth came down hard on hers, his tongue thrusting between her lips. With a shudder she opened herself to the sensual invasion and kissed him back. The heady taste of male hunger and rich wine attacked her senses. She dug peach-tinted nails into the lean, corded muscles of his shoulders as one powerful thigh slid between her legs. Her breasts were crushed against the solid wall of his chest and her nipples peaked in demand.

The hard door at her back and the rigid erection notched between her thighs contradicted the softness of his lips, the silky thrust of his tongue, the heady, spicy scent of his flavor making her drunk. For the first time, she thrilled in allowing her body to take over and be free to sink into every delicious sensation. Her senses exploded into overdrive until there was nothing to do but hang on and give him everything he wanted right back.

And she did. He swallowed her moan, and her hands wrapped around his shoulders, thrusting her fingers into the long, crisp hair at his nape. Her hips rocked with her own demand, until the simple kiss splintered into raw, primal hunger. His teeth nipped and he took the kiss deeper, until she turned into a wild thing in his arms, helpless against the wicked need for his tongue, his fingers, his cock. She twisted for more, and with a low growl, he cupped her ass and lifted her high, until her legs wrapped around his hips and she was a melting, boneless creature of lust.

She drowned in his kiss. She'd never felt so wanted, his hunger burning her alive—the sweet thrust of his tongue bringing an edge of tenderness that told her this was more than just physical. Arching upwards, she guided his hands to her chest. He muttered a curse and deftly released the buttons, pulling away the fabric to reveal the delicate lace camisole. His hands coasted over the lace, pulling it taut across her swollen nipples.

Caterina gasped. Her head fell back over his arm as his lips closed around the ruby crest, suckling gently. The delicious dampness of his mouth against her overheated skin, the silky touch of his tongue dragging across the fragile lace, both drove her into a frenzy.

"My God, you're burning up in my arms," he grated against her breast. She shuddered in response to his touch. "You taste so damn sweet. Let me inside. Let me show you how good we are together."

His words burned as much as his fingers dragging over her sensitive skin, but deep inside, a faint warning begged her to slow down. Lee was basically a stranger. What did she know about him? Enough to trust him inside of her home? Inside of her body?

No.

Not yet.

Slowly, reality seeped back, and she stiffened in his arms. He lifted his head and gazed into her eyes. "Caterina?"

She drew in a shaky breath. "I'm sorry. I can't."

Guilt started to build. She shouldn't have let things go so far. Cat braced herself for his response—anger, frustration, or maybe for him to pressure her to change her mind.

Instead, he cupped her cheek and smiled. "I understand. I'm sorry if I pushed too hard. You are hell on my self-control." He dropped a kiss on her lips, buttoned her blouse with gentle fingers, and stepped back.

Joy bloomed. He wasn't like other men she'd dated who focused on their own needs. This man cared about what she wanted. She smiled back. "Thank you."

"Can I see you tomorrow?" he asked.

She tried not to giggle like a lovestruck teen, but damned if she didn't see stars in her eyes as she blinked. "Yes."

"Good, I'll take you to lunch. Two p.m.?"

"Don't you have work?"

"Only in the morning. I want to spend the afternoon with you."

She nodded, not trusting her voice. She must have been staring at him, because his smile widened. "*Buona notte*, Caterina."

"*Buona notte*," she whispered.

She let herself inside and spent the night dreaming of tomorrow.

Chapter Six

"I bought you a present."

They stood outside in the square plaza, across from Café Brera. Rip took in the mischievous sparkle in those golden eyes. On cue, his heart did a tiny little skip, almost like a dance, and he groaned inwardly at the textbook cliché he'd become.

He was totally smitten.

Yesterday had been picture perfect. He'd pretended to work for half a day on mysterious property explorations, then met her for an afternoon excursion and long, lazy dinner. Thank God she'd stopped him the other night. He'd been so crazed with need for her, he'd lost his control. He refused to make love to her before Cat knew his true identity, even though the growing sexual chemistry between them was ready to explode. Still, he'd been ruthless in allowing her to set the tone of their intimacy. She had to seek him out in order to truly bind her in the way he craved. Physically. Emotionally.

Legally.

Edward had already warned he'd be calling her soon.

Time was running out.

He pushed the disturbing thoughts away and smiled down at her. She looked adorable in dark washed denim, a black, short leather jacket, and those teetering stilettos, today in bright pink. "Why am I suddenly worried?"

"I'm testing your ability to go with the flow today."

He crossed his arms in front of his chest and regarded her suspiciously. "I'm not the flowy type. I prefer control." He paused, his gaze resting on her lips. "In all things."

On cue, her cheeks heated. Curiosity stirred. The more he dug, the more innocent she seemed. He'd imagined her engaging in a long trail of love affairs in Italy, but she acted almost shy at times, as if she was unused to flirtation and the game of seduction.

"Oh! That's good. I mean, that's good to know."

He laughed. "I'm ready for my surprise."

"Okay, first I want to show you something." She stepped back, grabbing the opening to her jacket, and flashed it open. Underneath, she wore a hot pink T-shirt scrawled with the words, *Sex, Love, and Panforte.* "What do you think?"

The sweet curves of her breasts displaying that delicious message got him hard in seconds. He shook his head and shifted. Damn, he ached to strip off that shirt and bare her to him completely. Spread her thighs and bring her to orgasm with his lips and tongue and teeth, until she writhed and begged and screamed his name over and over and—

"Lee? Do you like it?"

The sweet way she uttered his middle name punched him in the gut. The guilt grew every moment they were together, until he realized he had to tell her the truth very soon. He got himself under control and re-focused. "Hell, yes, I like it. You look hot. Now, you have to take off the jacket." He dropped his voice. "Real slow."

Oh, yeah. She slicked her tongue across her bottom lip and those eyes heated up. She wanted him just as bad. It was time to break down some more walls today and ease her further into this relationship.

She shrugged the leather off, easing it over one shoulder at a time, slipping it from her arms in a deliberate tease. Then with a seductive smile, she threw the jacket at him, standing proud in a tight T-shirt and jeans that were sexier than any negligee. He loved it. Underneath the shyness was a bit of a she-cat. He couldn't wait to find out.

"Now it's your turn," she said. She rummaged in her bag and whipped out a black T-shirt, holding it open to display the motto: *Bread or Death.* "Do you like it?" When he remained silent, she broke into a worried babble. "I know, it's kind of stupid, right? Especially for a guy, but I saw it and knew you had this bread thing and thought it was going to be cute, but I'll take it back, it's totally okay—"

"Caterina?"

"Yeah?"

He took the shirt, an odd tightening in his chest making it hard to breathe. When had a woman ever given him a gift? Too long ago to even remember, and then it had been either generic or cheap. His fingers stroked the soft cotton and he looked into her anxious face, noting again that she was a giver, not a taker, so he did the only thing he could in the moment to show how he felt.

He kissed her. Long and deep and slow. His mouth cherished and pleasured with languid strokes until she softened in his arms and clung to him so sweetly he wanted to take her to his bedroom and show her how good he could make her feel. They kissed on the public street amidst the crowds and nothing ever felt so right. He pulled away slowly, her honeyed taste lingering on his tongue.

"*Grazie*. It's my new favorite shirt."

Her face lit up. "I'm so glad."

"In fact, I'm going to wear it right now." He handed her jacket back, and in one swift motion, peeled off his heather grey pullover. Ignoring the glances and stares of the various people surrounding them, he tugged on his new T-shirt, liking the way the cotton felt against his skin. "What do you think?"

Her jaw had dropped.

Amusement skittered through him. His woman seemed to like what he'd revealed, which made him feel like a fucking god. He wanted to strip off all his clothes and stand naked in front of her, relishing with pride the flare of lust gleaming from her amber eyes. Her gaze hungrily roved over his chest, his shoulders, and her fingers came up as if she wanted to touch him. Immediately, his gut clenched and the raw chemistry sizzled like a live wire between them.

"I think you're beautiful," she whispered.

Her honesty made him stiffen in agony. He blistered out a curse. "Keep looking at me like that and there's only one place we'll end up."

She tilted her head, as if considering it. He held his breath, but after a few seconds, she shuddered and stepped back. "I love the shirt."

"Good. Now that we're rocking the fashion world, what would you like to do?"

"Have you been inside the church yet?" she asked.

"No."

"It's been a safe place for me. I know it's a popular attraction, but I feel like it's just for me. Would you like to go in?"

He offered his hand and she took it without hesitation. "I'd like that."

They walked through the plaza toward the church of Santa Maria del Carmine. A dark metal statue stood in front of the church. Rip stared at the headless, armless sculpture with both interest and a tad of horror. The strange angular chopping of the body along with a small head sprouting from the chest hit an onlooker full force. Behind it, the faded brick of the church rose up in symmetrical matching halves against the dreary afternoon sky. Dual arched windows sat atop the door. A grand, detailed round window in the shape of a rose balanced out the structured architecture, leading to a carved cross sprouting off the roof. The church was smaller than most of the sweeping *duomos* of Florence and Rome, but a quiet peace pulsed around the building, offering welcome.

Cat guided him inside, where there were few visitors to navigate. Still holding hands, they made their way down the aisle, taking their time to admire the gorgeous detail of the altar, from the colorful frescoes of Jesus and Mary to the sweeping arch of the dome atop, surrounded by elaborate carvings of wood and gold amidst the sheen of stained glass. The textures and colors blended together in the art of sheer beauty, made even more majestic by the building's smaller, more intimate size. A hush fell upon the church and his humming nerves seemed to settle. It was almost as if his soul was finally able to take a long breath.

They were quiet as they studied the various frescoes, then took a seat in one of the pews. Rip had never been in a church other than the occasional sightseeing. He watched Caterina kneel, bowing her head with clasped hands, and pray. Her glorious hair masked her face in over a dozen shades of blond, catching the light trickling in. He sat and watched her, breathing in the damp air scented faintly of incense. Time passed. He reveled in the quiet and the presence of a woman he was beginning to care for.

Finally, she slid back onto the seat and smiled at him.

"What do you pray for?" he asked curiously.

"My father. Myself. The world. I pray I won't waste time on things that don't matter. I ask for forgiveness for craving expensive shoes when they don't even fit in my closet anymore."

He grinned. "Italian shoes can never be termed a sin."

"Finally." She gave a sigh. "A man who understands." She looked up at him with a beautiful smile. "Are you ready to go?"

He liked that she didn't push him for his religious beliefs or try to make judgment. She seemed to emanate acceptance with people, and Rip found it soothed his soul. "Yes, let's get something to eat." They walked out through the Piazza San Marco, enjoying the street market. They bought bowls of fish soup, and a hunk of crusty bread, and ate them on a bench, soaking in the atmosphere of the spring afternoon. Rip decided it was a good time to dive deeper. "Can I ask you a question?"

She glanced over. "Anything."

"The man you left behind in New York. The one who broke your heart. Do you still love him?"

She met his gaze head on. "No. For a long time, I didn't know how to function without him. We'd dated for so many years, it became more of a routine than a real love. He and my father were close, and it became easy to listen to them both. When I left, I realized I hadn't given myself any time or space to find who I really was. I'd become what they wanted. Does that make sense?"

It did. But another question swirled in his head, waiting for an answer. "Yes. But if you saw him, would you want to try again?"

She shook her head. "I never loved him the way a woman is supposed to love a man she's about to marry. He was a friend and a mentor. It was almost as if his role as a lover was secondary, and that's what I realized was missing."

Relief cut through him. He'd run into her ex-fiancé at a few social functions, but they kept their distance. From the stories Edward told him, Devon had not only been a cheater but a liar, too. Rip had discovered signs of embezzlement once he audited the books, but Edward refused to pursue retribution, choosing to move on and limit any future interactions. Rip was glad the asshole had shown his true colors to Caterina. The idea of them being married shuddered through him in pure distaste.

But he couldn't say any of it, so he settled on keeping it light. "They say sometimes the biggest fuckups make the most fortunate events."

She laughed. "You said that so much better than a poet. I agree." She finished the last of her bread and put down her bowl. "What about you? I know nothing about your past. Do you have a big family?"

Ice chilled his veins. He tried to act normal, even as the familiar distance leaked into his voice. "No. Just me."

She tilted her head and pushed. "Were you close to your parents?"

"You think you're better than us, boy? You're not. You're trash—and going to a fancy school with your fancy clothes and degree ain't gonna change who you really are."

The words of his father shook through his memory but he kept the wall firmly up. "No. I left for school and never saw them again."

A frown creased her brow. "I'm sorry. That's young to be on your own."

"I worked hard, did what I had to make it work. Got a full ride and graduated with a business degree. I was placed right away into an internship program and made my way to management."

"Ah, so that's where you got into property development, huh?" Her eyes twinkled and suddenly, Rip couldn't stand her believing a lie. He'd been wrong to lead her on with his mysterious statements about his job.

"I'm not in property development," he said. The words fired off his tongue before he had time to think it through. "I'm here for something else."

"What?"

"I'd rather not tell you right now. But I will." He nailed her with his stare. "Soon."

A flicker of wariness crossed her features. "It's not illegal, is it?" she finally asked.

His lip twitched. "No."

"You're not secretly married or seeing someone else, are you?"

He leaned over, placing his hand over her cheek. Her quickly indrawn breath told him how much his touch affected her. "There's only you."

"And you still don't want to give me your last name?"

He winced. "I promise I'm not a criminal."

"Witness protection?"

He groaned, trying to find a way to get her to trust him for a while longer. "This sounds ridiculous, but for a little while, I just want to get to know you without any of the other trappings or judgments. Does that make any sense?"

"Yeah, it does." She leaned in, happiness glowing from her. "Then I'll wait."

When she discovered the truth, she'd try and throw up barriers. Pretend they never had a connection. Convince herself to hate him. He'd take on the battle but right now, today, he wanted to savor the moment, wanted to soak himself in the purity of her presence, like the shadows chase the elusive flicker of the light. Wanted to believe he was the man who could make her happy.

"Let's go."

He stood up from the bench, threw away the garbage, and took her hand.

"Where are we going?" she asked.

He smiled. "Everywhere."

And they did. They wound in and out of the shops crowding the plaza and beyond, stopping at the Duomo, the Galleria, and the Museum of Art. They drank dry, sparkling Prosecco and ate honey biscotti and found a place to hide during the brief rainstorm that hit mid-afternoon. They stumbled on a tiny café with a few tables in the back garden, and ate dinner late at night, with the twinkling white lights strung on the trees surrounding them like an angel's halo. They drank red wine and talked of the things that made them happy, of great literature and movies that changed their world, and of the dreams that still lingered after they closed their eyes.

When he walked her to the apartment, he saw in her eyes she was ready.

But instead, he only kissed her goodnight, not trusting himself to hide the core of who he was from Caterina any longer, afraid she'd turn away if she knew the true darkness in his soul. He turned to go but she stopped him.

"Up for an adventure tomorrow?"

He absolutely refused to believe in the word giddiness. "Sure."

"Meet me here after your morning shift."

"I'll be here at one."

He left her with a smile on his face and a pit in his stomach.

* * * *

"I don't think I'm ready for this yet, Caterina."

"Don't be silly, we've fooled around enough. It's time to just do it."

"Maybe we're moving too fast." A worried tone seeped into his voice. "I think I need more practice."

"Nonsense. Keep your focus and let your body lead. You know the popular term, it's like riding a bike. Where do you think it came from?"

"I feel like an idiot," he muttered.

"Would you just do it? Slide your butt back a little more and adjust your leg to the left. Yes, perfect. Now, push!"

He took a deep breath and pushed.

With a whoop, Caterina watched him take off down the street on the bike, his hands wrapped around the handle bars in a death grip. "You got it!" she shouted, jumping on her own bike to follow. "Let's do this!"

"Are they going to stay out of my lane?" he boomed in demand. "Because I won't be able to stop."

The busy traffic of Milan wasn't the best place to teach a person to ride a bike, but she'd advised him to stay in his lane and keep his focus in front of him. Cat had been horrified to hear he'd never been on a bike. Had never learned to ride, even as a kid. Something inside her chest hurt when she thought of it. Even though he hadn't opened up, she felt as if there was a world of hurt within him that needed to be shared. Thankfully, she had taken advantage of the bike sharing program in Italy and knew the roads well. She'd just have to keep a sharp eye on him.

"Just focus on the road ahead and follow me. I'll lead us out of here."

Cars beeped, traffic jammed, and mopeds zipped in and out with an obnoxious roar. She clamped down on her giggle as she eased past Lee and noticed his usual calm, cool demeanor had been replaced with a touch of panic.

"You're doing great," she said as she rode beside him. "You're a natural. Just don't get in your head."

"There's a turn coming up so I don't have time to chat now."

"Lean into it like I taught you."

He did, barely swiping another rider who turned to give him a dirty look. "This is stupid," he muttered. "People should stick to cars, or trains. Hell, even a motorcycle makes sense. Why are we still using transportation that's powered by our own energy?"

"Bikes are the best way to get around in cities. Besides, don't you get a real sense of freedom and accomplishment? The wind in your hair, the sun on your face, the thrill of exhilaration?"

"No. I prefer air conditioning and a kick ass sports car."

She smothered a laugh.

"Too much technical development causes us to get lazy," she cheerfully replied, adjusting the small bag she'd packed with food and water.

He tossed her a quick glare, then re-focused on his crowded lane. "Did you just ride with no hands?"

"Yes, but I've had practice."

"Show off."

She laughed, giving him a tour as they made their way through the crowded city and headed toward one of her favorite spots—*Parco Sempione*. She kept a tight eye on him, hanging back to make sure he felt confident, and eased him out of the congested, city roads toward the famous Castle Sforzesco and the sweeping Arch of Peace. The historic brick castle stole her breath every time—the imposing tower holding central court, and boasting powerful defensive walls designed by da Vinci himself. Elaborate water fountains graced the front entrance, but it was the back of the castle Caterina sought—the true treasure being hidden.

"Let's park the bikes here and walk the rest of the way."

"Yes. Walking is good. Very good."

The road turned into cobblestones, bumping their bikes around, and she lifted her hand to point toward the castle. "If you look over there, you'll see the Castillo Sforzesco. We should get you a tour before you leave, but we're heading into the park for now and—uh, oh."

She realized her mistake immediately.

As a new rider, his gaze had been focused completely on the path ahead, and he'd refused to look left or right. But he'd automatically swung his gaze to follow her pointed finger. She held her breath as he coasted, but then the normal mental processes overtook him.

He panicked.

His hand jerked on the handlebars, the tires wobbled, and he crashed onto the sidewalk.

Cat stopped pedaling, hopped off her bike, and ran over to him. She pressed her fingers to her lips and focused all her efforts on keeping a straight face. "Oh, my God, Lee, are you okay?"

Slowly, he stretched out jean-clad legs from underneath the spinning wheel and looked up. The sun glinted in his coal-black hair. He pushed himself up and lay his palms on the rough cobblestones. The snug fabric of his T-shirt clung lovingly to every carved muscle. Those full lips tightened into a thin line. A faint chorus of Italian titters drifted in the air, and a few people stopped to grin at the crazy American sprawled out under his bike. "Don't even think about it."

Cat covered her mouth with her hand and tried to focus on something else. Unfortunately, the sound bubbled up at the back of her throat, demanding exit.

"One giggle. One tiny giggle and it's all over."

She flirted with the idea of jumping back on her bike to escape, but she had a feeling Lee would come after her.

A small boy stopped in front of them, peering over at Lee, then asked a question in Italian to his father. The parent shook his head and led him away.

"What did he say, Caterina?"

The giggle grew. "You don't want to know."

"Tell me."

"He said, 'Papa, did the big man fall down?'"

And then it happened.

She laughed.

In a flash, Lee jumped from the ground and tossed her over his shoulder in one easy motion. She shrieked wildly, laughing harder as he strolled leisurely toward the gurgling fountains, while the crowds pointed and smiled at them. With the backdrop of the brick tower, the two-tier fountain bubbled merrily and was a popular place for tourist pictures and tour groups to stop. Lee didn't seem to care about the audience as he stopped near the edge, near enough for a mist to hit her face in warning.

Holy crap, the water was cold.

"Umm, Lee? Can you put me down now?"

He ignored her, his hand solidly on the curve of her buttocks. "Hmm, I have no coins with me. If I throw you into the fountain instead, do you think my wish will come true?"

She froze. He wouldn't. Would he? "No! Your wish will most definitely not come true."

"But how can you be sure?" He pretended to toss her.

"No! Oh, please, please, I'm sorry I laughed!" She clung to him fiercely.

His deep laugh raked across her ears. "Yeah? How are you going to make it up to me?" He shifted her weight and shivers bumped over her skin. The intimacy of their position hit her full force. The weight of his arm splayed across her thighs, and that heavy palm pressed into the small of her back. Her breasts dragged against his solid back, teasing her nipples. Her face grew hot and her body grew needy.

"What do you want?"

He laughed again, but this time it was a sexy growl. "Oh, that opens up a whole boatload of possibilities. But why don't I just settle for a kiss?"

"Done. Can you put me down now?"

With slow, deliberate movements, he slid her down the front of his body. When her toes touched the ground, she was breathless and off kilter. It was his dark gaze locked on hers that centered her.

"You're mean," she said.

Suddenly, he snagged her around the waist and dragged her in. His fingers tangled in her hair and he tipped her head back. "You're pretty."

Her tongue came out to wet her lips. "Are you going to take your kiss?"

Triumph flickered across his features, along with an aching tenderness that stirred the nest of emotions buried deep. "No. I'm going to give you my kiss."

His mouth lowered, achingly slow, and he brushed his lips over hers. Once. Twice. Soft as a whisper, sweet as a song. Caught up in the moment, she leaned in and asked for more.

He growled her name and gave it to her. They kissed by the fountain, amidst the crowds, with the ancient tower keeping watch, and fell into each other. It was a kiss she'd never experienced before, full of possibilities, and when he finally broke away, she swayed drunkenly on her feet. They stared at one another for a few moments, a bit wary, as if they'd both realized something bigger had happened within that simple kiss and they couldn't go back.

It was the flare of panic in his eyes that made her blurt out the words. "That was a really good kiss."

A laugh burst from his chest, and he shook his head, grabbing her hand and pulling her away from the fountain. "Yes, it was," he said seriously. "But now I'm really hungry and I'm hoping you have something good in that bag of yours."

"I do. Let's get the bikes parked and walk to the *Parco Sempione.*"

They retrieved the bag, parked the bikes, and headed behind the castle. The pop of spring had brought out the crowds to enjoy the huge expanse of green lawn, leafy trees, and the glassy spill of the lake. A curved bridge led them over the water, and various paths wound through the trees to hidden sections of gardens with benches. The park was a treasure caught between the glorious Arch of Peace and the castle, a quiet, meditative place to think and appreciate the simplicity of nature.

She found a grassy space, laid out a picnic blanket, and opened the bag.

"This is beautiful," he said, studying the gentle slopes of green against the water and blue sky. "I guess when I think of Milan I don't think of parks."

"Think of the city. Central Park is quite beautiful, and they have their own zoo."

"You're right. Another reminder not to judge a city by its noise and population. We need to look deeper."

She shook her head and grinned. "I had no idea you could be a bit silly. I like that."

He looked shocked. "I'm not silly. I'm deep and broody, remember?"

"That's what I thought when I first saw you."

He propped up his arms behind him and cocked his head. "Okay, now I need to know. What exactly did you think when you first saw me? Please include the word hot in there somewhere."

She took out a small bottle of wine, two plastic glasses, and half a loaf of bread. "You reminded me of a dark angel. Sitting in the back alone in the shadows, focused on your drink. There was this silence that vibrated from your aura. I got the sense you could be surrounded by people but they wouldn't touch you. There was too much distance."

His chin jerked as if he'd taken a hit. She hesitated, not wanting to hurt him, but her gut urged her to continue. "When I looked into your eyes, I saw pain. It made me sad."

His voice flicked out like a whip. "Is that why you came over to me? Because you thought I was in pain and you felt sorry for me?"

She shook her head. "No. I came over because I felt something. A connection. It was like you drew me to you—into you—and that pain was just a part of who you were. That's why I love that you can be silly. That you almost threw me into the fountain, and agreed to ride a bike when you didn't really want to, and took your payment in a kiss. I'm starting to fall for you, Lee, and we just met. Does that scare you as much as it does me?"

He sucked in his breath, and she tried not to panic. Oh, God, she'd really put herself out there. And yes, she was a little embarrassed, but not enough to take it back. This man made her want things she'd never imagined before. She craved to delve into and explore every layer of him and open herself up again. She knew almost nothing about this man, yet her heart whispered she knew all the important things.

Would he pull back? Was it too much to ask after only a few days, especially when he planned to return to New York? Her heart pounded in an uneven rhythm while she waited for his answer.

"Yeah, it scares me. But no, I'm not walking away. How's that for an answer?"

She smiled. "It's perfect."

"Just one important thing."

She frowned. "What?"

"You still didn't mention hot."

She leaned in and kissed the delicious, sulky pout of his mouth. "Not just hot. Smoking hot. Blistering. Call a fireman sexy hot."

"Better. Let's eat."

She pulled out the chunk of hard parmesan, pears, and fresh honey. They cut off pieces of food and ate in the grass under the hot sun, fingers sticky, the fruity, dry wine chilling their tongues. Kids raced across the field, throwing rocks in the pond. Fat clouds floated by. Birds swooped in and out of the branches above and screeched in song.

"So how are you spending your time here in Italy?" he asked curiously.

"Are you asking me if I have a job?" she asked teasingly.

He laughed. "Do you?"

She popped a sliver of pear in her mouth drizzled with honey. "I've been thinking about launching my own purse line."

His brow arched. "I didn't know you were a designer."

"I'm not. I just got the idea recently to try something new. I've been taking some courses at Style Design college. I tried being a stylist for a while, then got into the marketing aspect of fashion but it didn't seem like the right fit. Design always intrigued me, so I decided to try and launch my own purse line. I got a job working a few hours at a local boutique. Sophia—the owner—introduced me to a few designers who were nice enough to answer some questions, so I'm slowly building some contacts. Once I have a solid line of samples, Sophia told me she'd let me try them out in her boutique."

"Sounds like a solid plan."

She blew out a breath. "It does, right? I feel like I should be further along, though. I worked hard my entire life, but when I came and settled in Italy, I had no idea what I wanted to do for work. It's harder when you have more choices."

"Definitely." He studied her intently. "Maybe you haven't found what you really wanted yet because you're meant to end up back where you started. Making wine. Maybe that's your true talent."

She wrinkled her nose. "I doubt it. But eventually, I have to do something. I tapped into my savings to finance this past year and a half, but the money is running out. I can't ask my father for more."

He looked away, and she wondered if he looked down at her for not having to work for so long. For being taken care of by her father, like a little girl. But she wouldn't be ashamed. She'd worked for that money just as hard, standing by her father night and day to learn and run the business. She had no regrets using the money to see more of the world and gain new experiences.

"I thought you'd be different."

Startled, she stared at him. "What do you mean?"

He waved a hand in the air. "I meant you're different from other women. You're very...honest."

"One of my downfalls. Why? Aren't you?"

He jerked and began stuffing the trash back into the bag. "I'm honest with myself. Here, let me get rid of this." He unfurled his long legs and walked across the lawn to dump the trash. She watched him walk with graceful strides, still giving off that air of isolation that was a part of who he was. Curiosity burned. She knew he was still hiding things from her, but he'd promised to tell her more very soon. Cat analyzed his last statement, sifting through the nuances, and finally caught a sudden realization.

"You're honest with yourself but not others?"

"Huh?"

She shifted onto her knees and faced him. "You said you're honest with yourself. Does that mean you lie to others?"

He shook his head. "No. There's just not a lot of people in my life to talk to. But I made that choice and I've been happy about it."

She studied the clench of his jaw, and the defensive gleam in his eyes. "Tell me a secret," she said.

"What?"

"A secret. We all have stuff we're keeping from others—the stuff that scares us. We drink or sleep or fall into bed with strangers or cry or make a love spell to avoid the consequences of our fear."

"Love spell?"

She pushed on. "It's a sunny spring afternoon. We're safe and happy and having a beautiful day together. Tell me one secret you've never told anyone else."

He looked at her like she was a creature from an alien species.

"Why?"

A smile touched her lips. "Because we can." He didn't speak, so she figured he'd opt out on her game. "Want me to go first?"

He took another sip of wine. "Okay."

Cat thought long and hard about which one to pick before she spoke. "I let my father push me toward a man he thought I should marry, a man I learned to love, but not with passion, not like a wife should love her husband. Even with the promise of owning my dad's winery, I wasn't enough to hold his interest. Will I ever meet the one who is meant to be mine? Will he love me for me? Will I be enough? So yeah, those fears are mine."

His stunned silence made her uncomfortable. Damn, she should have made a light-hearted joke afterward. She just wanted a way to connect on a deeper level with him, and he seemed so guarded about his past. About who he really was. Instead, he thought she was lame and kind of desperate and sad.

Oh, my God. What a stupid game to play.

Surprise hit when he grabbed her shoulders and looked into her face as if memorizing every feature and angle to bring into his dreams. "You are enough," he tore out raggedly. "You're amazing. Beautiful. Sweet. You're...everything. For a man. To love. One day. Do you understand?" He shook her slightly. "Caterina?"

Her eyes widened and she choked back sudden tears. Where had this man come from? She swallowed hard and nodded. "Yeah. I understand."

His hands dropped away like he'd been burned. He turned and muttered something under his breath. "Maybe we should go." He moved and this time, she grabbed at his arm. "I'm sorry, Lee. I shared too much, too soon. You don't have to tell me anything at all. This was a perfect day."

She pressed a kiss to his rough cheek, and got up from the ground. Brushing the grass from her jeans, she folded the blanket and turned to go.

"My father once beat me because I got straight As in school." He spoke casually, as if this was a normal conversation. She stilled, clutching the blanket to her chest, and waited. "Said I was a fucking show off. Told me to never forget where I came from, because I could study in a fancy school, and get a fancy job, and a fancy girlfriend, but inside, I was trash and it would always come out. I'd never be good enough for the life I wanted."

The horror hit her, but before she could respond he went on. "At first, I didn't want to believe him. I figured the harder I worked, the more I accomplished, I'd leave everything behind and show him good. One day, he'd beg me to acknowledge him as my father. I'd have money and success and all the things he'd warned me I couldn't get. But he died before I graduated. He died before I could prove it to him. That's one of my biggest regrets. That I couldn't look the son of a bitch in the eye and show him who I was."

Instinct made her reach out to take his hand, entwining her fingers with his. She waited, sensing there was more. "What about your mom?" she asked.

"Ran out on me when I was ten. Heard she got a nice new family with a husband who doesn't beat her. Probably doesn't need me to remind her of the crap she left behind." He stared at the ground. "The funny thing is I think that asshole was right. I watched others snatch up internships from high family and political connections. I watched cliques form at the country club that had always made me feel fake and uncomfortable. And I've always felt like an outsider, no matter what success I've accomplished. So that's my stuff. The demons, as you'd term them."

She looked into his eyes and realized there were no words of comfort to ease a past that had hurt him so deeply. So, instead, she stepped into his arms and offered him the comfort of her body, then told him the only truth she knew, right here and now.

"It doesn't matter what happened before," she said softly. "You're enough, too."

He hugged her back, tentatively at first, then allowing himself to relax into the embrace. They held each other for a while under the warm sun, until they slowly broke apart, leaving their hands still clasped.

They walked out of the park and back toward their bikes in silence, but something had shifted again between them, piercing the thick wall of secrecy surrounding him, exposing a few shards of truth to the light.

For Caterina, it was enough for now.

* * * *

Later that night, Rip shot out of bed, his lungs gasping for air.

Fighting back a shudder, he rolled off the mattress, his skin damp with sweat. He glanced at the clock.

Midnight.

Fuck.

He hated when the nightmares came. Occasionally, they'd rise up from his subconscious, like gleeful little devils reminding him he hadn't outrun them. Whenever he'd begun to succeed and build confidence in his abilities, his father's voice danced in his head in its familiar, taunting tone. Whenever he hoped someone would spot worthiness for love in his soul, her mocking laughter would drag him back down to the pits of hell.

The conversation with Caterina had let them loose.

He hadn't been able to stop thinking about her.

You're enough, too.

He got up and shrugged on jeans and a T-shirt. Went to the bathroom and splashed cold water on his face; brushed his teeth. He'd never had a more perfect day. After the park, they'd gone to dinner, and on to *La Dolce Famiglia* for dessert. Instinct had pushed him to tell her the truth that night, but she'd cited a morning appointment with a purse designer, and Rip sensed it would be better to leave. The kiss at her front door promised much more, very soon. He'd quickly texted Edward when he got back to the hotel and asked for a few more days. He still hadn't heard back.

Rip looked in the mirror and wondered what Caterina saw in him. Eventually, she'd realize he was a fraud, a man who'd lied about his identity. A man who'd never loved or been loved in return. A man who wanted things with her he'd never thought possible.

His lungs tight, he couldn't breathe; he needed air. Stumbling out the door, he headed down to the lobby, through the doors, and took to the streets.

His life had been a long string of successes and failures, but he'd never questioned if he was happy. Growing up with a father who hated him had taught him never to seek such a luxury. No, life had been about survival, pure and simple. He'd learned early any type of reaction incited more attention from his father—usually left in black and blue marks. It hadn't taken long for him to master masking his feelings and remaining distant, cold, untouchable. But inside, the mass of raw emotion simmered dangerously. School was his ticket out, and he'd taken the violence until he graduated and left before he exploded into a rage of hate that would destroy him.

He remembered the first time he'd met Alicia. She'd been the first woman he'd fallen in love with—a woman with class and breeding—from her expensive sports car, designer clothes, to the wicked restlessness gleaming in her hard blue eyes. She'd brought him home to the family vineyard and announced her intention to marry him.

Rip saw his job as a new opportunity to prove himself. His enraged future father-in-law cut him down at first, but grudgingly found that he had a raw talent with the grapes, a rare palate and skill with blending that quickly had him moving ahead.

His boots ate up the uneven pavement and he fought with the memories. That first job had taken patience. Timing. He'd sought comfort in the endless acres of vines that needed constant care and attention. Under delusions he had found a family, he'd bought a ring and proposed under a moonlit sky, in the vineyard, on bended knee.

And she'd laughed. Told him she'd never intended to marry him. She'd just been looking for some fun, intending to piss off her father in the process. She'd craved his body, his brooding savagery, but not the man he was inside.

Once again, Rip had learned the lesson.

He was alone.

When he began working for Winsor Winery, Edward offered him hope. Over the months, they'd bonded, and Rip believed he'd finally found a home. He'd dreamed of running the business with Edward's full support and approval, never expecting to be pushed to marry his daughter. Once again, he'd allowed himself to believe he could be part of a family. Once again, he would be turned away. Never enough.

His body shook. A low, animal groan ripped from his lips. He stopped and looked up.

Moonlight spilled over her window, illuminating the endless flowers bursting from the wrought iron balcony. Was that a light burning inside or his imagination? It didn't matter. Somehow, he'd ended up here, his subconscious pushing him where his heart wanted to be.

With Caterina Winsor.

He needed to bury himself inside her tight, wet heat. Feel her cool fingers travel over his body. Needed one night of raw, honest passion before he told her the truth; before she turned away from him and put her walls up. He wanted her open and sweet, surrendering to everything he could do to her and give her.

He stumbled forward as if in a drunken haze. Rang the bell. Waited.

The light over her door flicked on. Footsteps echoed. The chain of a door released, and she peeked through the crack. Her eyes widened. He heard a quick intake of breath.

The door opened wider.

He stood before her, hands out, and gave her the only truth he could.

"I need you tonight, Caterina." His voice was both a plea and a fierce demand. "The demons are here."

Seconds ticked by. The air seethed with savage emotion.

Slowly, she stepped aside and let him enter.

Chapter Seven

One look at the depth of emotion in his eyes and Caterina knew that tonight she would become his.

He needed her. The jagged, sharp edge of hunger and pain carved out the lines of his face. A haunting agony gleamed in those inky dark eyes, urging her to reach for him and soothe away the ache. It was time to take a leap with her heart and hope Lee would catch her.

The door shut behind him. They stood in her entryway, both of them silent, a need-filled energy pulsing around them. His eyes locked on hers and he reached out his hand, asking for her complete surrender. Without hesitation, Cat slid her hand into his.

With a low groan, he enfolded her in his embrace. His hard, heated length cradled her curves. The sensual energy crackled and churned between them. Then his mouth crashed down on hers and staked his claim.

She needed no urging this time to part her lips for him, allowing him full access. She met each silky thrust of his tongue with her own demand as he dove in and out of her mouth, as if starving for her taste. Her fingernails bit into his muscled shoulders and she arched upward for more, losing herself within the intensity of the soul-stirring, demanding kiss.

He tore his mouth from hers, breathing hard. "Bedroom?"

She swayed on her feet and jerked her head toward the right. "There."

He lifted her into his arms and strode through. The quilt was covered with roses, and her sanctuary spoke to the most deeply feminine part of her, from the antique four poster bed, pearl encrusted mini chandelier, to the make-up and vanity mirror with the beveled silver mirror. He pressed her onto the mattress and stared down at her like a conquering warrior. Heat surged between her thighs. His hand trembled slightly as he reached out and caressed the length of her body. Usually shy, she suddenly felt sexy and empowered to make such a powerful man tremble.

With one easy motion, he pulled off his T-shirt and threw it on the floor. Her mouth dried up as she stared at his gorgeous build, jeans hanging low on his hips, a virtual painting of lean sculpted muscles and smooth olive skin, of dark whorls of hair dusting his chest and disappearing into the waistband of his jeans. Never taking his gaze from her face, he flicked open the button and pushed the denim down, leaving him clad in black briefs. He removed a package from his pocket and threw it on the bed. Then he paused briefly before stripping naked and kicking his underwear to the side.

Dear God, he was beautiful. He radiated a masculine grace evident in his carriage and the proud tilt of his jaw. She drank him in, every sloping muscle and hard angle, every inch of his throbbing cock that was hard and ready for her. Then he put one knee on the bed, dipping the mattress, and loomed above her.

"I've wanted you from the very first night," he murmured, tugging his fingers through her hair, touching her cheek, his touch as gentle as his voice. "There's a connection between us. Do you feel it?"

"Yes." She caught his hand and dragged it to her breasts, arching upward. "I've wanted this, too."

He tugged down the spaghetti straps of her black slip. Cool air hit her flushed skin, tightening her nipples, and his eyes glittered as he slid a palm over the peaks, rubbing back and forth to wring a moan from her lips. "Oh, the things I want to do to you," he said in a husky voice. "Things that make you moan. Things that make you scream. Things that make you beg for more."

She shuddered, gripping his wrists as he pulled the fabric down until it was bunched around her waist. Her skin burned, and the aching, wet need pulsed between her thighs. "I want you to do them all. It's just that—" She broke off, embarrassed to tell him the truth.

"What is it?" His voice gentled even as his eyes blazed like lit coals. "Too fast?"

"No, I just don't—I just don't want you to be disappointed." Oh, God, that was a humiliating admission to utter. She craved to duck her head and hide from her lack of experience, but forced herself to continue looking into his face. They'd come too far to pretend now.

He stiffened. "You're not a—?"

"No! But I've only been with one man, and he felt it necessary to cheat on me with another woman. And now I'm going to die of humiliation." Her face felt hot, thinking of all his experience in the art of seduction, and how little she really knew. Her ex had treated her like a delicate doll, and they'd never had a robust sex life. Another reason his betrayal had rocked her world—believing she hadn't been enough for him in bed.

"Don't." The command blasted from his lips and made her gasp. He leaned over and pressed his forehead to hers, his hands cupping her breasts. "He was a weak asshole who never deserved you. And I'm glad there have been no others. I can't wait to show you all the delicious things you've been missing. I'm glad I'm the man to watch you shake and shatter beneath me. *Capisce?*"

Relief and a sense of lightness flowed through her. "*Capisce.*"

"Now, let me get back to work." He nibbled on the edge of her jaw, then dragged his tongue down her body in slow, torturous increments. The heat of his breath teased each inch of skin he explored. He nipped and licked and kissed her body until liquid fire poured through her veins. Her breasts swelled and her belly tightened.

"Please," she tore out. Her hands clenched in the tangle of sheets as he moved lower, desperate for him to stop, desperate for him to continue.

"Please what?" he drawled. His fingers traced the line of her thigh.

Her legs jerked and tightened. "Don't tease me anymore."

With one swift motion, he rose up and pressed his body over hers. His erection throbbed with demand at her core. His muscled thighs pinned her legs. His hair-roughened skin slid over her sensitive flesh and her toes curled at the delicious contradiction of hard and soft, rough and smooth, heat and coolness. Midnight eyes gleamed with sensual demand. His lips tugged in a masculine smile. "You haven't given me enough yet. I want more—much more." He took her mouth again, thrusting his tongue deep.

"Open your legs for me." He growled the words against her mouth. She shuddered as he nipped at her bottom lip, and slowly parted her thighs. His fingers gently traced the golden nest of hair, teasingly, until one finger dipped into her swollen heat. He tested her, moving in and out with slow, playful movements until she gasped for breath, rocking her hips for more. "Wider. Let me see all of you."

She groaned out his name, finding his demand shameful and hot, and obeyed. He murmured his approval as he drank his fill, his finger playing her like an instrument. Wetness leaked down her thigh and her body wept for relief from the tightening, excruciating ache. "So beautiful. All sweet and swollen and pink. You are a fucking goddess."

"Lee."

"Tell me what you want."

She closed her eyes and dug her nails into his muscled arms. "You. I want you."

Coal-black eyes gleamed with fierce satisfaction. His mouth took hers in another soul-stirring kiss as he pushed three fingers deep into her channel, thrusting with a hard demand, relentlessly pushing her toward the edge. His thumb rubbed her clit with light, teasing touches, keeping her in a sensual agony, and then he bit her bottom lip and flicked her clit hard.

The dirty command raked across her ear. "Come."

His fingers curled and thrust. She screamed and writhed beneath him, the orgasm rushing through her body. His mouth never left hers, swallowing every choked cry, his fingers never stopping until the last bit of pleasure was wrung from her shaking limbs.

With one smooth motion, he pushed her thighs up, spreading them wide. The crinkle of a wrapper rose to her ears, and suddenly his hands grasped her wrists and pinned them above her head. Blinking, her head deliciously fuzzy from her orgasm, Caterina looked into his seething eyes and sensed that once he took her body, nothing would ever be the same. Jaw clenched, his erection poised at her dripping entrance, he paused for endless moments.

"You belong to me."

With one swift thrust, he entered her body, burying himself deep inside her tight channel.

Claimed.

The sheer power and size of him stretched and burned inside her. His hard, muscled chest crushed the swell of her breasts. His fingers interlaced with hers as she gripped tight, struggling to accept the masculine invasion without giving him everything she had.

But he wouldn't let her. As if he knew her thoughts, he withdrew from her clinging warmth with slow movements, then drove inside once again, keeping the teasing, tantalizing pace at a steady rhythm. Her head arched back into the pillow as her body demanded more.

"That's right, all of it. Don't hold back."

The tempo increased to a frenzy, until a scream hovered on her lips. Skin damp with sweat, his gaze never left hers, commanding her to surrender.

Her body shuddered and she let go. Waves of pleasure washed over her and she gave up completely.

She heard his hoarse shout as he followed her over the edge, and then he collapsed, tucking her in and holding her tight. His hands gently stroked back her hair, cradling her against him with a cherished tenderness that made her soul sigh and relax completely. As she drifted off to sleep, one thought danced in her mind.

This was a man she could love.

* * * *

"Good morning."

Cat blinked drowsily and stretched. Her hair lay out on the pillow like a glorious, tangled halo, and her skin was flushed a dark pink from sleep. A crease from the pillow left an imprint on her right cheek. The scent of sex and musk hung heavily in the air.

A strange joy flooded him, and Rip couldn't help but lean over and kiss her, her lips soft and full and sweet under his. In one night, this woman had changed him. He'd never been with someone who opened her heart with welcome, the same way she gave him her body with a purity that humbled him. This wasn't just about sex. It was about all those other emotions sliding and sinking together inside him that made him feel terribly vulnerable and hopeful at the same time.

After only a brief time, he knew the truth.

He was falling in love with her.

"Is it time to get up?" she murmured sleepily, her fingers running down his stubbly cheek.

"Not yet. I'm going out to grab some cappuccino and pastries. I just wanted to let you know where I was going."

A smile curved her lips. "So I don't wake up and assume this was a one-night stand?"

"You know this is more, right?"

The smile slipped away. She pressed a thumb to his lips. "It is for me. I'm glad you feel the same."

Guilt churned. He fought it back and squeezed her hand, then pressed a kiss to her palm. "Good. We'll talk when I get back. I have some things to tell you."

"Your mysterious job?"

"Yes, and other things. But first I need caffeine."

"Sounds like a plan. Think I'll stay right here and wait for you to get back." Her mischievous wink got him hard and ready, but he managed to step back with a tortured groan, enjoying her bubbly laughter. He headed out of her apartment, stopping briefly to look at the arrangement of roses on the table.

He'd sent the arrangement last week. Only four remained, carefully pruned by her loving hand. Strange that she'd never mentioned them...or the mysterious message that had accompanied their delivery.

Foreboding ruffled his nerves. He shouldn't have sent the roses. Hadn't realized the game would end up real for both of them. How would he convince her of that once she learned the truth?

Rip walked to the café. Edward had called him this week, asking for an update. Rip refused to explain any details, assuring the man he'd be returning with Caterina soon. Once there, he'd convince Edward that Caterina was much more to him than a way to gain the prize of the winery.

She had become the prize.

But first he had to explain everything to her this morning.

As he stepped into line, Rip practiced the words he would soon say out loud and prayed they were the right ones. Prayed that Caterina would believe he'd fallen in love with her because of the wonderful woman she was and not as a means to an end. Prayed that they could be happy together.

Rip repeated the words like a mantra.

Chapter Eight

God, she was so damn happy.

Caterina got up from bed to brush her teeth and comb the tangles from her hair. Her body felt achy and well used. Her face held a touch of beard burn. Her lips were swollen.

She looked like a woman who had been treasured and fucked like a queen.

Laughing with joy, she headed back to her bed, propping up some pillows against the headboard and lying back. Eyes closed, she pictured every image of last night in slow motion. They'd connected and bonded completely, on a deeper level than just physical. She was ready to take the next step if he asked her.

She was ready to go back to New York. With him.

Her bliss was interrupted by her phone. Seeing her father's number, she accepted the call. "Hi, Papa! I can't believe it, I was just thinking about you and coming home."

"I've missed you, sweetheart." His booming voice over the line brought comfort and an ache. "I wanted to see how you were."

"Actually, I'm wonderful."

A pause. "Really?"

She laughed at the doubt in his tone. "Yes, I'm happy. I met someone, and if things go well, I may be coming home."

He sucked in his breath. "I cannot believe it. Do you have true feelings for Rip? He wouldn't tell me anything and I worried about you. Worried I'd pushed too hard and demanded something you couldn't give. I sensed you two would be good for one another, but this is a true gift!"

A strange roaring filled her ears. She gripped the phone and sat up in bed. "Rip? No, his name is Lee."

"Lee? What do you mean? Dark hair, tall, dark eyes. You're talking about Ripley Savage, correct? The man you fell for? He's my partner at Winsor. He traveled to Italy to bring you back home so you can take your rightful place at the winery."

The room spun, and suddenly, her world flipped. Her lungs constricted and she gulped for a breath. "Papa, I want you to tell me everything. Right now."

He did. As he spoke and the horror unfolded, she realized she'd been a pawn in a very complicated, high stakes game. The prize was Winsor Winery. The sacrifice was her.

Again.

Rip Savage had managed to trick her, ripping apart her already tattered heart in the process.

Her voice tore from her throat. "I can't believe this. Not again. I have to go, Papa. I'll call you later." Caterina closed her eyes and fought for control. Rage and hurt swirled through her body, begging for release. It all seemed so clear now. The roses with the strange message. Coincidentally meeting him at Bar Brera. Dear God, she'd walked right into the trap without pause. She'd actually introduced herself to him! And he'd played his part well, allowing her to believe what they had was real, all the way up until last night. Had he been planning to propose this morning? Had he figured to sweep her up into the romance of an elopement, then spring the truth on her when it was too late?

A moan escaped her lips and she shook her head. So stupid. She'd been so stupid to think a man could fall for her so quickly. He must've been laughing at her the whole time. Maybe he was laughing right now, congratulating himself for his seduction skills.

She jumped out of bed, frantic to get dressed and put a barrier between them. Flinging on jeans and a T-shirt in a panic, she heard the door bang and footsteps clatter. His voice drifted through the door. "I hope you didn't move, because I'm planning a picnic in bed. I figured— Caterina? What's wrong?"

She froze, then slowly turned to face him.

When her gaze met his, he sucked in a breath. The truth pulsed between them amidst the tangle of lies, and she watched as a curious pain ravaged his features. For one brief moment, his dark eyes held a raw grief and regret that slammed her in the chest, but then she reminded herself it was all fake, and hardened her heart once again.

The white-hot anger turned to numbness. Grateful for the relief, she tilted her head and regarded him in silence. He whispered her name, taking a step forward.

"My father called. I know everything. It's over and I want you to get out." The words dropped like a hard stone between them. She lifted her chin. "Now."

Rip stared back, his face rigid. Growling under his breath, he closed the distance between them in three long strides. "It's too late." He leaned in. His warm breath struck her lips with each deliberate word. "Caterina, don't do this. You're everything I want in a wife. We belong together."

She tried to move but found herself frozen in place. She steeled herself against the sheer menace of masculine power and held her ground. "Not anymore," she flung out. "Not ever!"

He fisted his hands at his hips, his posture rigid. "What did he tell you?"

"Everything!" she shouted. "The truth! You came to Italy with one mission: marry me. I can only imagine how pleased you were I fell right into your trap. You pretended to be a man I could care about. How far were you willing to go, Rip? Or is it *Lee*? Quite a clever ruse. Were you going to propose this morning?"

He swore viciously under his breath. "I know you're furious right now, and I understand why. But if you hear me out, you'll see nothing's changed between us."

Her eyes widened. "You can't believe that," she said. "I would never marry you."

"What happened between us has nothing to do with the winery, or your father. Yes, I came here with a plan because I had no choice. Don't you understand I was desperate? I was promised a stake in your father's company and worked my ass off to get it. Then I find out there's a catch. In order to get what I deserve, I have to marry Edward's high society daughter, who ran out on him and his business. The daughter who cared nothing for her father's financial trouble." His laugh held a touch of bitterness.

"Wait a minute. Winsor Winery is in financial trouble?"

He spoke in a calm, controlled voice. "Caterina, the winery was on the verge of bankruptcy when I stepped in. Your father was all alone and sinking fast. We worked night and day to turn it around, and the whole time he spoke of how you were traveling through Europe without a care in the world. Imagine the impression I had of you. A selfish, spoiled princess."

Nausea rolled in her gut. She shook her head hard, trying to deny it. "No, he would've told me. Papa said we had plenty of money to finance a trip and that I didn't need to work."

"He lied. He knew how fragile you were and that you needed the time away."

"I can't believe this," she whispered. Everything she'd believed true had been a lie. She fought the urge to crawl under the covers and cry. To hide from the world and cocoon herself from the pain. To hide and run to safety.

But she was done running. The past year had shown she was stronger than she believed, and one heartbreak would not ruin her. Drawing on her strength, she squared her shoulders and faced him head on. "I see. And you wanted your stake in the winery enough to marry a self-centered brat you would never respect?"

Direct hit. He winced and took a step back. "You don't understand how important Winsor Winery is to me. I've been working toward owning something my whole life. I figured if I could get you to fall for me, I could tempt you to come home with the promise of an easy life."

"You bastard," she whispered. "You judged me before we even met. And I fell for your stupid plan. Have you been mocking me this entire time? Was this seduction planned out in detail?" Furiously, she fought back tears, shattered at the idea of him being amused at the open vulnerability she'd exposed.

He walked toward her but she jerked away, throwing her hands out. "No, I hadn't even decided how to approach you when you came up to me in the café. You felt our connection. I felt it too, drawing us together before I was even ready. The moment we met, I fell hard. You were nothing like I expected, but I was still so angry with your father and the situation, I kept thinking you'd show your true colors. Instead, every day you surprised me. I came to you last night just as a man. I craved you, needed you more than my next breath, and I could never regret making love to you. It meant everything."

"It was a lie," she said.

"The only lie was my true name. Everything else was real." His eyes blazed with emotion. "My body, and my heart, was yours last night, and still is yours. If you'd just—"

"Don't." She whirled around, refusing to look at him anymore. "And the roses? That was you, too?"

"Yes."

"Good move. Women are suckers for a bit of mystery."

"I'm sorry, Caterina. I can't change how we began, but I'll be damn sure to fix how we go on. We can be happy together, I know it. You can plan the wedding, here in Italy or back in New York. Anything you want." When she didn't respond, he added, "Accept the inevitable. We will be married."

"Never," she whispered. "The man I gave myself to last night was good and kind. He made me feel safe. He needed me." She stared out the window, her voice bleak and emotionless. "You're not that man at all. You're ruthless and cold. You believe in sacrificing anyone who gets in the way of your goals. And I could never love a man like you."

A hushed silence fell over the room. She refused to look at him, knowing if there was any pain in his eyes she was stupid enough to want to soothe him, even after she knew the truth.

"I'm still the man you fell in love with," he said quietly. "Still fighting for the life I want, for the woman I want."

"I don't believe you anymore," she said. "You lied and made a mockery out of my feelings. It's over." She motioned toward the door.

"Think, Caterina," he said, refusing to leave. "Your father is tired. He can't run the winery any longer and needs to retire. His health hasn't been good—another thing he's been keeping from you. I know the business. I can run it and make it even more successful, and if you'll marry me, I can keep it in your family for generations to come."

Guilt assailed her. The thought of her father sick, stressed, and alone while she happily lived like a society princess tore at her. Oh God, had Rip been right? Had she been so focused on herself that she didn't want to see the issues, happy to be blinded by her own selfishness? It had been easy to lean on her father and believe him when he urged her to take some time away from the winery.

Too easy, perhaps.

"Fine, I will return home. But I'll get my father to teach me everything I need to know." She threw her head back with challenge, glaring. "We don't need you."

"Your father will never trust you to run the winery alone. And he'd never retire if he knows you're struggling."

"I'll hire people," she said desperately. "I can do this without you."

"But you don't have to." His velvet voice stroked her ears. "When I took you to bed last night, it wasn't about playing games or trying to secure the winery. It was about you and me. I meant every word I whispered, when my body claimed yours. I swear I can make you happy, if you give this a chance. Please give me a chance."

She stumbled back, desperately needing the space. Even now, her traitorous body leapt and responded to his emotional plea. The images flickered before her, memories of caressing hands drifting over her skin, of low murmurs whispered from carved lips, of hard muscles covering her body and bringing her to heights she'd never experienced.

Heights she would never experience again. At least, not with him. He was a liar. A manipulator. A user. He was not a man to trust. And yet, for all her father had sacrificed...how could she not sacrifice for him? He'd sounded so happy on the phone when he talked about her and Rip being together—and relieved she was coming home.

"I'll go home with you. I'll agree to an engagement while I convince my father to change his mind. But this will be an engagement in name only. We'll have separate lives. Separate bedrooms."

A muscle worked in his jaw. Slowly, he lifted his hand as if to touch her, then dropped it back to his side. Those eyes swirled with raw emotion, but it was the sadness that tore at her heart. How could he have possibly believed they would end in happily ever after?

In a split second, his demeanor changed. He straightened to his full, impressive height, shoulders back, his focus unwavering. "Then I'll just have to change your mind, won't I?" He swiveled on his heel and walked away. "Pack up. We leave tomorrow."

"I need more time."

"We've run out of time. And don't think of running away. If you do, I'll never stop looking for you, and that will only put more strain on your father. He needs me back at the winery, Caterina. He needs us both."

The quiet click of the door echoed in her ears. Mashing her fingers to her lips, she sank back down on the bed and did the only thing left to do.

She cried.

Chapter Nine

The car crept up the winding hill, past the wooden sign welcoming them to Winsor Winery. The silence between them grew so loud, Cat's ears began to throb, but she didn't care. She kept her gaze stubbornly trained out the window and refused to acknowledge his presence.

Yesterday had been full of chaos and tears. She'd visited *La Dolce Famiglia* to say goodbye to Mama Conte with promises to visit Michael once he settled in New York. Her beloved apartment was left bare, her belongings packed up in boxes and shipped off. She told no one about her impending marriage, still in a daze at the chain of events that had upended her safe little world.

The worst part?

Finding the carefully folded paper under her mattress from the spell she had cast. Her soul-mate couldn't be a liar and a deceiver, but unbelievably, she realized her list hadn't included honesty. How could she have forgotten to specify honesty?

Holding back a sigh, she watched as the endless trees dropped away to reveal the magnificence of the mountains in the distance. A mass of carved rock dominated the skyline, shimmering in the light with an arrogance and power that reminded Cat of a queen on her throne.

She caught her breath as Rip stopped at the top of the road and cut the engine. Her gaze swept the familiar surroundings and a shiver raced down her spine.

Home.

Endless acres of rolling land lay before her, spreading as far as her gaze could reach. Vines now dotted the landscape, which looked like an attempt to try growing some of their own grapes. They'd purchased extra land years ago, but every time she suggested harvesting their own grapes, she'd been voted down by her ex. Instead, Devon had been obsessed with having extra seating and set up a large eating area with picnic benches and a small garden. Personally, Cat thought it was a waste of important space, but she'd been outvoted. Seemed like Rip had finally convinced her father to try.

The graveled pathway led up to the stone mansion, and she blinked away the memory of her father standing on the porch, overlooking his land with prideful eyes. As a child, she would sit atop his shoulders as he toured his kingdom, instructing her on the proper way to blend the grapes. Her education had been strict and relentless. But her father had taught her the secret to success, which demanded more than a first-class education and textbook knowledge.

It required love for the land.

Respect for the grapes.

It demanded soul. Passion. Patience.

Heart.

Her father had trusted Rip with his cherished business. Did he believe Rip possessed such qualities? He must—or why would her father insist she marry him?

The confusing questions swirled in her mind, but she caught sight of her father—his tall frame and thinning white hair a familiar beacon. Dressed in his black business suit, spectacles perched on the end of his nose, he exhibited his usual polished demeanor, yet seemed much thinner. Her heart stopped and she was dragged back in time, staring at the man who had raised her, taught her, protected her, and loved her with his every breath.

She threw open the door, hurrying up the path until she stood in front of him. Mixed emotions raced through her, but his joyous smile and open arms broke through her resentment, pushing her forward. The security of his embrace along with the scent of Old Spice washed over her with a wave of comfort. Tears burned her eyes as she clung tight. She spoke against his chest. "I missed you, Papa."

"I missed you more," he said gruffly. "I'm so glad you're home."

Footsteps over gravel rose to her ears. She sensed a presence behind her, along with a brooding type of energy, but she didn't turn around. The trip here had been positively painful with strained silence neither of them seemed able to break.

"Rip, thank you for bringing her home."

Cat raised her head and snorted. "Really, Papa? Are you seriously thanking Rip right now?"

Her father shot her an apologetic glance and patted her shoulder. "I know I have much to explain, my sweet girl. But I'm happy to see the two people I love together."

Rip cleared his throat. "I'm going to walk the grounds and get caught up."

Edward nodded. "That deal you worked out with Silver Vineyards paid off. Our orders of Chardonnay are up by eighty one cases from last year. Sal is in the tasting barn with the new event schedule, and the deliveries are confirmed for this Friday. My daughter and I will be inside for a while having an overdue heart to heart."

She refused to glance at Rip but felt his gaze boring into her back. "Very good."

More gravel crunched and she relaxed as Rip walked off alone. Her father patted her shoulder. "Come in, love, I have some coffee on."

They walked through the bright blue door and she took in the surroundings with a smile. Beautiful plank wood floors were covered with colorful braided rugs, and a huge brick fireplace was the centerpiece of the main room. Beamed ceilings, antique built-ins, and leather furniture completed the homey, yet rich look, softened by various knick-knacks and childhood pictures from her school days. Cedar barrels held various wine bottles along the walls, and the scent of wood smoke hung in the air.

A staircase led to an upper floor with an open balcony. She glanced up, wondering what Rip's room looked like, then followed her father into the kitchen. She slid onto the stool, leaning her elbows on the Tuscan swirled granite, and stared at him. "I'm angry, Papa."

"I can only imagine." He filled two mugs with coffee, added a splash of milk, and brought them to the counter. "I'd like you to hear me out."

"Why didn't you tell me you were sick?"

"I'm not sick." His pale blue eyes filled with apology. "I'm just tired. The doctor recommended a warmer climate and easier lifestyle. It's time I retire."

"Fine, then retire. I'll run the winery."

His sigh was filled with regret. "You're the rightful heir but you've been away almost two years. Rip has been able to expand our client base, arrange new contracts with vineyards, and build back our profit margin. His relationships are key, and if he walks away, we risk losing all those new contacts. Rip saved the winery. He's become more than a partner to me—he's like family. He deserves to own a piece of this winery just as much as you do."

She shifted in her seat. Frustration rushed through her. Coming home and seeing the land she loved had reminded her how much the family winery truly meant to her. She would not walk away again. And yet, staying meant she'd have to marry Rip, unless she could come up with another option.

If only her thoughts weren't complicated by the strong, conflicting emotions Rip had brought to the surface during their sensual, loving night together. She'd actually started to consider a future with him. But the ache of betrayal still burned inside of her chest.

How could she marry a man who lied so easily—one she could never trust?

"Then sign over a share to Rip and leave me with the controlling majority. There's no need for marriage."

Edward tapped his finger against the rim of the mug. Her heart tugged. He did look tired. His elegant face was more deeply lined, and those bright eyes had dulled. He'd definitely lost too much weight. His body seemed frailer. He'd always been a robust, dynamic man who claimed a room once he walked in. He must be extremely weary to finally agree to leave the business he loved. "Winsor Winery was built on family who ran the business together—a true partnership beyond paper. As much as I love Rip, I've been entrusted by the generations before me to keep the Winsor control to one hundred percent. Marriage is the only way to guarantee you both share the winery."

Her father faced her with a pleading gaze. "Cat, I've thought about this for a long time. Rip is a good man. He's nothing like Devon, who I'll never forgive for hurting you, and breaking my trust. Rip has something that I don't see much of anymore— integrity, and the need to make his mark the old-fashioned way. Reminds me of one of those old John Wayne movies, where the cowboys were rough around the edges but had some damn honor. The two of you are well suited."

She studied her father, so wise, so loving, such a good judge of character. What did he see in Rip that she could not?

Rip had made her feel things she'd never believed possible. He'd sworn to her his feelings were pure. With time, could she learn to trust him again? Forgive? Rebuild their connection so she could sift through what was real and what was fake?

Confusion swamped her. "I want to help you, Papa. I just don't know if this is the right decision. I'm not ready to marry someone I can't trust with my heart."

He reached over and grasped her hands. "Then spend more time together. Get to know each other better and try working as a team. I'll stay on a bit longer to help."

Her mind churned. Finally, she tilted her chin up and gazed at her father with determination. "One month. At the end of that time, if I prove I can run the winery on my own without Rip, and still don't want to marry him, you give me full ownership."

A frown creased his brow. He stared at her for a long while before slowly nodding. "I never want to see you unhappy, Cat. If you truly don't feel you can love Rip, and can run the winery alone, at a profit, I agree. But I want you to try to keep your heart open. You deserve a man who is worthy of you. Give Rip a chance to show you who he really is. Can you do that for me?"

She swallowed back the lump in her throat, refusing to feel guilty about denying Rip the ownership he so badly wanted. But she needed time to decide and see if she could truly run the winery on her own. To remember what had first drawn her to him. To figure out what, if anything, was real between them.

"Yes, Papa. I promise."

* * * *

Cat followed the twisting path down the hill. The sun sank low on the horizon, throwing the valley into a streaming silhouette of fiery colors. She leaned against the trunk of a large weeping willow tree and let the peace of the Hudson Valley wash over her, soothing her nerves. Her gaze swept over the grounds. Twisted vines newly budded with grapes thrust skyward against the backdrop of the Shawangunk Mountains. Rich brown soil melded into a soft carpet of green that spread out in endless acres. The outbuildings and main barn housed the heart of the operation—the blending cellars and the tasting room where she'd spent most of her formative years.

The air charged, and a quiet presence pressed down upon her. She closed her eyes halfway, trying to ignore the prickle of energy that sprang loose in her body at his nearness. The delicious scent of soap and musk drifted to her nostrils. He stopped beside her, hands in his pockets, staring out at the valley. "How did the talk with your father go?"

"Fine. We agreed to delay the wedding for a month."

His shoulders stiffened but he didn't glance at her. "Giving you time to change your mind?"

"Giving us both time to figure out if this is what we want."

"I don't need any time. I already know what I want."

Anger slapped at her. She forced the words from between gritted teeth. "Winsor Winery."

"And you. Always you."

A shiver bumped down her spine. "My father's going to stay a while. There's a lot I need to learn. I think it's important to see if we have a chance at a real partnership."

"And a real marriage."

The words dragged like velvet against her ears. She remembered her promise to her father, and nodded. "Yes."

He turned to face her. The sun glinted in the coal black of his hair, throwing his profile in sharp silhouette. She studied the angular, proud lines of his face, the slash of his nose, the heaviness of his brows. His entire aura pulsed with masculine power and intensity. "You'll agree to a truce? Allow me to show you what we can be to each other, beyond the winery?"

Her heart squeezed at the possibility of them having a fresh start. "I can't promise anything. What you did in Italy will be hard for me to forgive. But, for my father, I'm willing to give you a second chance."

His smile startled her as much as the words he spoke in a gentle tone. "Then I'll prove to you what we have is real."

Her heart stuttered. He was an intoxicating puzzle of tenderness and savagery, always throwing her off balance. But she'd promised one month and she intended to keep her word. "We need to go slow."

"Of course. Can I take you on a tour? Show you all the changes we've implemented?"

"Yes, I'd like that."

He reached out his hand and waited. She stared at those strong fingers, open and waiting, then slowly placed her hand in his. Her belly dropped at that first gesture of trust, but he didn't push for more, just led her down the path toward the tasting barn. "Your father said you were able to recognize a fine vintage at age twelve. You have a gift."

A small smile touched her lips. "The Winsor blood powers my taste buds. I grew up racing barefoot across these fields and studied winemaking when other children were learning their ABCs. It's part of my history."

"A history you ran from. Do you regret being pulled away from Italy and the new career you wanted to launch?"

"I regret the circumstances," she said honestly. "But being home feels right."

He squeezed her hand. "I'm glad. Let me show you the main tasting room first. We decided to expand." She walked into the familiar barn and blinked in surprise. It was gorgeous. He'd torn down the back wall and built an impressive bar of rich cedar, with elegant red stools and a large eating area made out of barrels and hand carved wooden tables with benches. One corner held a souvenir shop filled with glasses, shirts, bottle stoppers, and an array of interesting goods. The space was easily double the size, with an organized flow that would lead guests to either individual or large group tastings. "We launched a menu of wine and cheese pairings, and sell picnic baskets for lunches. Our event schedule offers a band for entertainment and themed weekends that have been hugely popular."

"This is amazing," she murmured. One entire wall was stocked with endless bottles of wine in an elegant art display. "What are your average numbers for a spring weekend?"

"Over two thousand."

Her mouth fell open. They'd courted only a quarter of that number before she left. "Fascinating. We always relied on old-fashioned word of mouth and our stellar reputation, but I knew we lacked a strong marketing effort."

He nodded. "Unfortunately, the competition with other vineyards on the wine trail, Angry Orchard, and breweries cut into our traffic. I initiated a brand new marketing plan for weekend tastings and began booking tour buses for groups."

"What outlets did you use?" she asked curiously, running a hand over the smooth cedar bar top.

"Groupon has been quite successful. We booked a local band who's been looking for exposure and has gotten popular. We built up our showing at all local events—the county fairs have been hugely profitable."

She moved to the open door, staring at the plot of land filled with twisted vines, set deep in the valley away from the barns. "And the vineyard? How is that working out? I've always thought it would be a good idea to try and harvest our own grapes for a small vintage," she murmured. "My ex told me it was silly."

He gave her a fierce frown. "We established your ex was an asshole. Your father told me about it and I thought it was a brilliant idea. We didn't need the garden or eating area placed there, so we shifted everything around. We're hoping to have our first successful harvest next spring. We also introduced a brand-new Riesling that I think will give Brotherhood Winery some competition." His voice lifted with an enthusiasm that intrigued her.

She cocked her head. "They've served their Riesling at the White House. It's one of the best."

"Ours is better."

The pride etched in his voice hit her full force. She stared at him, taking in the glow in his obsidian eyes and the satisfaction in the set of his face. The evident passion he held for Winsor Winery touched her deep inside, uncurling a slow flood of heat through her bloodstream.

He seemed to love the land as much as she and her father did. As if there was a connection that burned bright—a respect for the grapes and the process her father had consistently repeated as the foundation of true success. It went deeper than the simple call for profit. Wine demanded dedication. Precision. Fervor.

Emotion.

The realization slammed through her and stole her breath.

"Do you want to taste it?"

She jerked, her gaze focusing on those carved lips. Her belly did a slow tumble. "Taste it?"

A gleam of amusement danced in his dark eyes. "The Riesling."

"Oh! Yes, I'd love to taste it. Later." She ducked her head to hide her heated cheeks, but caught his low chuckle. Damn. She needed to re-focus. "Have you done any other renovations?"

"We're in the process of building another structure to host larger gatherings and parties. I think we're missing a lot of income from events, but it's been slow getting that segment of the business started. I've been slammed with work and the wine always comes first."

Energy buzzed through her as she looked at her surroundings. The familiar blended with new and gave her a whole new outlook on Winsor. The possibilities seemed endless, especially when viewed through Rip's gaze. No wonder her father didn't want to lose him. He'd become part of not only the day-to-day workings of the winery, but its vision for the future. She nibbled at her lip, understanding so much more now, realizing how much had changed during her absence. Wondering where she fit in with her own family business.

As if he caught her thoughts, he tipped her chin up with a thumb and stared into her eyes. "Caterina, I want us to work together on all these plans, but I also don't want you to feel forced into doing anything you don't want to. You left because you had no choices. This time, you do. Whether you keep designing purses, or take on the blending or tasting events, or marketing, I don't care. I want you to be happy."

He seemed so sincere. Her throat tightened, and she nodded, a bit overwhelmed by the sheer volume of change she'd experienced in the last forty-eight hours. She stepped back, needing the space. "Thank you. I think I'd like to get settled in my room. Peruse the new website and catch up on some things."

"Of course. I've left your things in the adjoining bedroom to mine."

Her voice pitched. "Adjoining? What about my old room?"

"There was a slight water leak in your room, so your father is having it re-painted and renovated. This one has the biggest master bath on the opposite side of the house. I figured you'd want some privacy and space." He paused. "The door between us locks, of course. Until you decide you want it open."

A shiver raced down her spine. She tried to answer, but found the words stuck, so she managed a nod and a full retreat.

God knew, she desperately needed to regroup.

Chapter Ten

One week later, Caterina took in the massive crowds scattered over the grounds and grinned with satisfaction. Lively music drifted in the air, and the picnic tables were filled with families and couples eating and drinking wine. The day was hot and bright, and the last bus tour was scheduled to leave within the hour. Hopefully, things would begin calming down.

Her gaze sought out Rip, who'd been working nonstop since six a.m. He stood framed in the entrance of the barn talking to Sal, a fierce frown on his face. Dressed in dark washed jeans and a button-down white shirt, he exuded the confidence of a leader and a quiet intensity that showed his work ethic. For the past week, she'd studied the spreadsheets to learn about the new pricing system, met and cemented relationships with all the employees, and re-learned the workings of the winery under Rip's leadership. Every day brought a new challenge, and she was surprised at how much she loved waking up in the morning, a sharp focus energizing her.

The door stayed closed between their bedrooms, but her heart was beginning to open with every encounter.

He was endlessly patient and generous with his time, making sure to show her every change he'd instituted and listen to feedback. But it was more than that. It was the light in his dark eyes when he looked at her. The gentle sweep of his fingers over the curve of her cheek. The deep laughter he let loose in her company. Once again he'd become the man she'd known in Italy, opening himself up to her with a relaxed ease that urged her to do the same. Sure, the sexual chemistry danced and burned between them continually. But it was the bond of friendship they'd begun to form in the past few days that held her heart captive.

Shaking off her thoughts, she walked over to him. "What's the matter?"

"I booked a three p.m. tasting for Sal with an important client. Do you remember the Wallaces?"

She frowned. "They own Riptide Vineyards in Westchester, right? Do we still bottle their Merlot?"

Rip nodded. "Yes. Their orders have doubled in the last six months. Bob has been wanting to come out for a visit. He decided to bring his family over today and I have everything set up. We have the pairings ready, extra baskets of cheese and fruit, and a batch of the chocolate truffles. He just neglected to mention one important thing."

"What's that?"

Rip let out a groan. "That he was bringing a dozen of their nieces and nephews and none of them are old enough to drink."

Caterina spotted the giant swarm moving toward them and sucked in her breath.

Holy crap.

The adults looked as if they were going to a high society tea party. The men were dressed in khaki twill shorts and freshly ironed shirts, and many sported fedoras. The women were a vision in white: white linen shorts, white silk tops, white sandals, and white hats. They approached in a beautiful vision of glamour Cat could only admire.

Until the line broke.

A bunch of children charged from behind and ran down the hill, shrieking at the top of their lungs. They were all different sizes and shapes, but they all charged with the spirited determination of youth. Two tumbled to the ground and rolled, regardless of the crowds in front of them or the weak disciplinary cries from the adults. These children would not sit quietly at the table and wait for their parents to drink their wine. These children would need focus and attention.

These children would need a serious distraction.

Cat shared a glance with Rip. "We have apple cider and soda tastings to offer," she said with a touch of desperation.

"That will hold them for five minutes. We need a plan."

"Okay, you get them set up at the table while I raid the shed. There are some balls, frisbees, and old toys in there."

She turned but his hand shot out and grasped her upper arm. "Please hurry. I'm not—I'm not good with kids. At all."

Cat nodded. "Be back in five."

She raced away as fast as her Prada sandals could go.

* * * *

Rip stared in horror at the group of children before him.

He'd faced down his abusive father, taken a brutal beating by some local bullies who'd jumped him, and pitted his negotiating skills against the best CEOs in the state.

None of that had terrified him like eight children waiting to be entertained.

After he'd gotten Bob, his wife Tracey, and their extended family set up with Sal, he'd taken the children to a separate area in the back corner of the tasting room. It had taken them approximately five minutes to gobble down the extensive collection of snacks, cider, and soda he'd offered them.

Of course, he'd told Bob and Tracey not to worry, that he'd keep an eye on the kids so they could enjoy themselves. Naked joy sprung to all the parents' eyes when they found out they'd scored a babysitter on a Saturday afternoon so they could drink wine.

What the hell had he been thinking? And where was Caterina?

"This place is boring!" the chubby blond boy with the spiked hair commented.

"We can play tag," one of the little girls suggested. She was dressed in white denim shorts with a floral T-shirt that declared *Princess* on it. She had blue lips, and her hands were covered with blue marker.

"Do you have Xbox or Wii U?" asked another dark-haired boy with a Spiderman T-shirt on.

"Or a TV so we can watch *Sofia the First*?" a little girl asked softly, her big brown eyes wide and innocent. She was dressed in a yellow Beauty and the Beast gown with a hole in the skirt. Dirt smeared her plump arms. "Or *Beauty and the Beast*? Belle is my favorite. Who's yours?"

He knew one, thank God. "Cinderella."

Her eyes lit up. "Good choice!"

"Thank you."

"I want to go home," the first boy announced, his brows slamming together like a little old man. "I want my mom and my 3DS."

"I have to go to the bathroom," another boy said.

"Hey, let's go pee in those tree things," the other boy yelled, pointing his finger at the window.

"No, I'll show you the bathrooms! We don't pee in the vines."

The Belle girl sighed. "They like to pee everywhere," she said solemnly. "Girls can't do that 'cause we have vaginas. It's not fair. Hey, will you have a tea party with me, Mister?"

"Yes, you can be the queen because boys can do girl stuff and girls can do boy stuff," the other little girl said with importance. She had pigtails, crooked teeth, and wore a T-shirt with a sparkly cat on it.

"Can I borrow your phone to play Angry Birds?" another boy asked.

Rip wasn't sure, but he thought a whimper escaped his lips.

Suddenly, like an angel swooping down, Caterina arrived, carrying a large box with different stuff poking from the top. The kids immediately stilled, surrounding her like she was a female Santa.

"Okay, everybody," she announced. "We're going to play outside. We'll start with Capture the Flag and break up into two teams. Girls against boys. Prizes will be toys from the box."

"Is that Star Wars?" one of the boys yelled.

"Maybe," she sang, blue eyes twinkling. "First, Capture the Flag. Then we'll empty the box and play."

"Cool," the dark-haired boy said.

"Yay!" the girls shrieked.

Rip tossed her a grateful look, and she winked back. They headed outside the barn to the far corner of the vineyard, and she chattered nonstop with the children about endless silly subjects they seemed to enjoy. Rip trudged behind her, grateful to give her the lead, and thinking about what a wonderful mother she'd make one day.

His chest tightened with a strange emotion.

Almost like longing.

Longing for something he'd never wanted with any other woman.

* * * *

An hour later, after several rousing games of Capture the Flag, a few Simon Says, an epic Hide-and-Go-Seek game, and more snacks, Rip finally collapsed under a tree. The kids were busy with pitchers of lemonade and cider, and plates of cookies laid out on the picnic table.

He was enjoying his lemonade and a few minutes of rest, when the youngest girl, Emma, floated over to him. She had blond flyaway hair as fine as silk, along with wide brown eyes. "Can we play tea party now?" she asked sweetly, reaching out to tug his hand.

He blinked. "You don't want to play with the toys?"

She shook her head. "No, thank you. You're the queen. What do you want your name to be?" she asked.

"Umm, Charlie?"

She giggled and shook her head harder. "No! It has to be a girl's name!"

"Oh, okay, how about Sophia?"

She gasped. "Just like Sophia the First!" she squealed. "Stay there. I'll get your crown and the tea stuff."

Rip watched Caterina swoop a Stormtrooper into a full-on battle with Luke Skywalker and his band of rebels. The boys were all gathered around her, bashing toy figures and making cool noises. Slowly, the other three girls drifted over to him. "Whatcha doing?" asked the nine-year-old in the princess shirt. He'd finally learned her name was Amber, and she'd proudly recited her age many times since she was the oldest.

He refused to allow his cheeks to heat up. "Having a tea party with Emma."

"Cool, I'll help." Amber sat down with her sisters, Ellen and Sharon, and stared at him. He shifted his weight and swallowed. They kept staring. He cleared his throat.

Emma came running back. "I have your crown!" she announced, her hands full of grass, yellow flowery weeds, and some pussy willows. "Queen Sophia, how do you take your tea?"

He tried to speak in a manly voice. "Just straight."

She'd picked up a bunch of plastic cups and the last of the cookies. Settling down in the circle, the girls all surrounded him, doling out cups, pieces of cookies, and trying to construct a crown.

"Queen Sophia!" Emma announced. "It's time you crown us your royal subjects and give us our titles."

"I want a good one," Amber said.

"But first you need to wear your crown," Ellen chirped. "Lower your head."

He glanced at his wrist watch and realized he wouldn't be saved for another half hour. Then he bent his head to accept the tangle of weeds and brush that barely formed a circle. Immediately, his head itched and he wondered about tics or crawly bugs going into his ears. When he faced them once again, all their faces were filled with joy and wonder, as if he'd literally transformed into a queen in front of their eyes. A strange emotion coursed through him, and he wondered what it would have been like to believe in magic as a child, to be cared for and loved and protected, to feel free to be silly and adventurous and believe in his imagination.

He wondered how it would feel to be safe with someone you loved.

"You are now queen of the trees and the land before us," Emma said softly.

"How may we serve you?" Ellen asked.

He stared at the girls, who waited for his answer.

Oh, what the hell.

He looked over and grabbed a stick from the ground. "First, I must properly knight each one of my loyal subjects," he said seriously. "Princess Emma, I crown you the animal whisperer. You may now communicate with all the animals in the land." He touched both of her shoulders with the stick, and her gasp made him bite back a smile.

"Princess Amber, I knight you Protector of the Light. No darkness or shadow shall reign in your presence."

"Cool," Amber murmured.

He went down the line, knighting each of the girls. After they each had their special jobs, they indulged in tea and cookies, chattering about the ways to protect their land without war or guns or as Emma termed it—mean stuff.

He didn't notice the shadow falling over them until he looked up and met a pair of whiskey eyes.

"What are you doing?" she asked, her voice husky.

"Playing," he said simply.

It was then he realized he could lose himself in her gaze—a treasure chest of pure golden light that would fight off all the shadows.

He could find himself in her gaze.

"It's time to go. I just got a text from Sal the tasting is over."

"Okay." He raised the stick high in the air and faced his subjects. "Queen Sophia officially calls this tea party and strategy planning to an end. Do not forget to be loyal and brave subjects to save our world. We are counting on you."

He carefully took off the crown and rose to his feet. Emma grabbed one hand and Amber grabbed the other, and he listened to their easy chatter back to the tasting barn.

Chapter Eleven

Something had changed.

Caterina walked toward the blending room, seeking out some silence and solace. Another week had passed. Seven days, where she'd spent most of her waking hours with Rip, learning the day-to-day requirements of the winery. Seven days of feeling torn between running Winsor on her own, something she now felt capable of doing, or running it with Rip.

The dynamics between them had started to shift. Her anger had started to fade, and in the short time since she'd returned home, Cat found herself falling for him all over again.

Watching him with those little girls, wearing a grass crown with pride, throwing himself into their game with pure intentions—that had touched her heart.

Working together had given her a glimpse of what their life could be like—professionally as well as personally. She'd discovered a routine she relished, which worked in perfect complement to what Rip excelled at. For the first time, she felt needed. She felt like she'd found a place she belonged to all over again.

On her own terms.

Today's delivery had shown the kindness of the man who might one day be her husband. She'd opened up several boxes to find a mass of materials—supple leather, exquisite beading, buckles, and clasps, and an amazing array of accessories to design her handbags. The envelope had included only his signature.

And one perfect red rose.

Caterina sighed and stepped down into the cellar. Breathing in the familiar cool, dank air, she passed the steel vaults holding valuable grape blends and endless oak barrels, all marked in a strict timeline. As she made her way farther down the halls, another scent rose in the air—a scent she was beginning to crave on a regular basis. The scent of man and soap and musk, uniquely his.

"Were you looking for me?"

The gravelly voice stroked her ears and tumbled her belly. She eased deeper into the dim light and found him perched on a low barrel, a few glasses by his elbow. Three bottles were lined up and uncorked in front of him. He wore the black T-shirt she'd bought him declaring *Bread or Death*, and the snug fabric hugged his broad shoulders and chest. His powerful legs were stretched out, and he regarded her with a lazy predatory ease that made her heart stumble. His fingers clasped the stem of the glass, and Caterina remembered the glide of his hands over her naked body, the sheer strength combined with a shattering tenderness that blasted through her defenses. His dark eyes flared, as if he'd caught the same memory.

She cleared her throat and took a few steps forward. "Nice shirt."

His lips tugged up in a half smile. "One of my favorites. Reminds me of you."

The simple words cut deep, past the carefully built barriers of her heart. She shifted her weight, fighting the need to go to him and hold him close. "I wanted to thank you for the supplies you sent. That was very thoughtful."

He arched one black brow. "You're welcome."

A short silence settled between them. The finely tuned sexual tension stretched tight. She pulled in a breath.

"I don't want you to feel like you were forced to give up your dreams to return home. Have you been happy working at the winery?"

She blinked. It was rare anyone ever asked if she was happy doing anything. Caterina pondered his question. "Yes. It feels different this time. The changes you instituted give the place a freshness and new energy. Actually, I wanted to talk to you about the additional structure being built. I think we need to think bigger than parties. A wedding venue on our grounds would be a huge draw here. I'd like to speak to an architect about installing a permanent overhang so we could have ceremonies and receptions without worry about weather. What do you think?"

He cocked his head. "I think it's a great idea. I've been interested in expanding to weddings but haven't had the time to take it on."

"I could reach out to a few architects and get some plans drawn up with costs. Then reach out to some local caterers to see what types of packages we could offer."

"Yes. But I'm slammed with other stuff—can you run with this?"

"I'd love to."

"Then it's your project. Just let me know how I can help."

Satisfaction rushed through her. Rip trusted her. The past two weeks had shown he valued her opinion and wasn't just trying to humor her when she brought up new ideas. For the first time, she felt like Winsor Winery truly belonged to her. It was a precious gift.

And this man had given it to her.

"Thank you." They stared at one another. Awareness surged between them. "What are you doing?" she finally asked.

"Taste testing. You came at a perfect time." He lifted the glass, swirling it around. "I need you to try this competitor's wine and tell me what you think."

She cocked her head, studying the intense frown on his face. Her hands itched to smooth the crease away, run her fingers down his stubbled cheek, trace the sulky curve of those lips. She swallowed, smothering the hot bolt of sensual attraction that tugged at her belly and softened her sex. "Sure."

His voice dropped. "Come here."

She closed the distance between them on shaky legs, reaching out for the glass he'd been swirling in contemplation, already making note of the splash of the legs against the sides. He took her by surprise by lifting the glass and pressing the rim to her lips. "Close your eyes," he demanded softly, and automatically, she obeyed. "Smell."

She took a deep breath. Blackberry. A hint of currant. A touch of orange.

"Now, drink."

He tilted the glass and she drank. She held the cool liquid in her mouth for a moment, allowing the flavors to warm, letting her Winsor palate take over. Her blood heated as the florals took hold and tried to take her on that glorious slide of pleasure, but it was suddenly over and everything went flat.

Her eyes flew open.

"What do you think?"

His eyes were so dark, seething with a passion that stole her breath.

He looked at her like that every day, his gaze hungrily roving over her, but it was the tenderness that always shook her to the core. The gentle touch of his fingers when he pushed her hair from her cheek, or the intimate smile when he caught her gaze across a room, or even when she'd stumbled in those Gucci heels and he'd carried her back to the house, insisting she change her shoes so she wouldn't get hurt. He was overprotective and domineering, yet kind.

"Caterina? What do you think?"

She blinked, trying to surface. "It's good."

His lips tugged slightly upward. "Anything else?"

"The blend is full-bodied and complex. But the flavors are short-lived. It needs…" She broke off, struggling to put her thoughts into words.

Rip bent closer. His lips hovered inches from hers. "More?"

An explosion of heat rocked through her. A whirling array of images flickered in her vision. Images of his hands over her skin, whispering demands in her ear, thrusting into her body as he commanded she give him more…

"More what, Caterina?" he asked. His hand traced the line of her jaw, down to her beating pulse, over her shoulder, across the swell of her breasts. Her heartbeat thundered at the light strokes of those talented fingers. Her nipples hardened and pushed against her blouse in a demand to be freed. "Tell me what you think it needs."

Her voice was ripped from her throat. "More passion." She trembled, caught on the precipice of backing up and moving closer. "More richness." Her tongue slid along her bottom lip to catch the last ruby drop of liquid. An animal groan escaped his chest. "More heat."

The silence pulsed with unspoken demands. Slowly, he placed the glass down. She caught the tremble in his hand and knew he was just as affected, the crackling sexual tension ready to ignite between them. He cleared his throat. "Very good. Now, I want you to taste one of ours. It's a new blend I've been working on." He handed her a bottle of water and she drank to cleanse her palate. Then he took the other bottle of wine and poured a new glass, duplicating his motions. She noticed the legs were stronger on this one, the rhythmic swirl of the liquid almost hypnotizing. "Close your eyes."

She obeyed.

"Smell."

The aroma rose to her nostrils. Like the first, she scented berries and currant, but there was an undercurrent of smokiness—mixed with a hint of dark chocolate. The complexity was heaven to her nose.

"Now, taste."

The rim was pressed to her lips and she opened her senses. The ruby liquid slid over her tongue and burst into bright florals of deep berries. This time, the flavors softened as she held it in her mouth, and the smooth smokiness lingered, stretching out into various notes as she swallowed. The tannins were rich without a bitter aftertaste, and she immediately craved another taste, her brain scrambling to make sense of the beautiful tones.

She opened her eyes. His gaze burned and ate her alive, and without thought, she lifted her arms to grip his shoulders. "The aroma seduced me."

"And? Tell me more."

She shuddered at his raw, almost carnal demand. "This time, the flavors lingered. It started off bright and fresh, then turned darker and more intense."

Her nails bit into hard muscle. A groan ripped from his lips. "Did my blend give you more? Did it give you what you crave from a wine?"

She tipped her head back with an open invitation. Intense hunger exploded in her belly, traveling like wildfire through her body, heating up her blood. "It was real," she whispered. "The first promised but didn't deliver."

His palms rested on each side of her head as his mouth descended. His breath rushed warmly over her lips. "You're right. Our competitor held back. When the winemaker is afraid of being overwhelmed by raw form, the product will be flat. On the surface the wine will look normal, but the trick will be discovered the moment someone tastes it. The emotions may have been avoided, but the product will be lifeless." His voice shook with promise. "I would never make such a mistake."

His mouth stamped over hers.

He kissed her with all the pent-up passion that had been building over the last two weeks, thrusting his tongue deep inside and gathering her taste. She clutched at his shoulders and matched every demand with her own, her nails sinking deep into his muscles, opening her mouth wider for him.

He pulled her tight against him, his hands cupping her ass and lifting her onto his lap. Her legs wrapped around his hips, his erection notched between her thighs as he kept kissing her, deep and hard, his tongue claiming her with every fierce stroke. "I've missed you so damn much," he muttered, nipping at her bottom lip, then soothing with his tongue.

"I've missed you, too," she admitted, arching back with invitation, desperate to touch and taste every part of him. He pressed kisses down her neck, biting the sensitive flesh, and she slid her hands under his shirt to stroke his hair-roughened chest, reveling in each hard muscle that jumped under her touch.

He muttered something under his breath—either a curse or a prayer—and rocked her against his erection. She squeezed her thighs tight and buried her face in his neck as every muscle in her body tightened with the aching need for release. His hands stroked her back, cupped her breast, tweaked the hard nipple, lighting every part of her on fire, until an itchy, empty hunger burned.

"Need more," she gasped, her hips rolling with her own demand. "Please."

He growled her name, kissing her deeply, and worked his hand down the front of her jeans, his fingers just touching the lacy edge of her underwear. "My God, you're on fire for me. So sweet, so perfect. I have to touch you."

"Yes, touch me, Rip—"

"Caterina? Ripley? Are you down here?"

She froze at the sound of her father's voice. Rip cursed, his hand shaking as he withdrew and quickly slid her off his lap, righting her. With adept, gentle fingers, he fixed her tousled clothing, then gave her a burning look. "Your father has terrible timing," he said, frustration nipping at his voice. "Stand in front of me."

She dragged in a shaky breath and tried not to sway on her feet. "And if I move?"

"Your father's going to get a big surprise."

A giggle escaped her lips. His face softened, amusement curving his lips, and she raised her voice. "Papa, we're in here."

"Oh, sorry to interrupt. Are you tasting the new Merlot you blended, Rip?"

"That's right. I was getting Caterina's opinion."

Her father glanced at both of them, his blue eyes lighting up with a joyous satisfaction. "Good, very good. I just wanted to tell you both I'll be gone for the weekend. My friend Daniel invited me to stay with him at his vineyard in Long Island. He knows I'll be leaving for Florida soon, so I wanted to make the trip while I'm still here."

"That sounds like fun," she said, smiling. "Tell him I said hello and hopefully we can have him over for a visit."

"Sounds good. Now I'll leave you alone to finish your wine tasting."

Cat glanced over. The banked promise of finishing what they started gleamed in Rip's inky eyes, and suddenly she panicked, needing the space. It had only been two weeks and already her emotions ran deep. Each encounter she spent with her prospective husband solidified their connection and pushed her closer to admitting she was falling in love with him all over again. If she took him into her bed, she'd have no place left to hide.

She had to be completely sure.

"I'll go with you, Papa," she said, quickly joining his side. Rip frowned, but didn't call her back. "I have some things to finish up. I'll see you later, Rip."

She turned, but his gravelly voice rose in the air with an intimate promise.

"*Presto*, Caterina."

She shivered, her mind flicking to the image of one perfect red rose, then Rip's determined face.

She didn't look back as she raced up the stairs with her father safely beside her.

* * * *

She was still running from him.

Rip uttered a curse and paced in the darkness of his bedroom. A few nights ago, he'd sensed her opening up to him in the cellars, and when he'd kissed her, she'd practically burned up in his arms. He knew if he'd pushed, he'd be sinking between her thighs and buried in her sweet, hot heat. He dreamed of the tiny cries she made at the back of her throat when he kissed her, and the way her hands trembled when she touched him, almost reverently, making him feel like a god. He craved her like his next breath. She was slowly driving him insane.

But he'd sworn to give her time. He never thought he'd want anything as bad as Winsor Winery—the ultimate symbol of achievement and success in a world that had mocked him.

Until Caterina Winsor.

He realized he wanted her more.

Rip glanced at the clock. Almost midnight. She wasn't coming to him tonight.

Slowly, he walked over to the adjoining door and pressed his palm against the wood. Struggled with the need to push it open and seduce her into admitting she loved him. Each day, he watched her soften and open up more. Each day, he hoped she would look in his eyes and realize the truth of his feelings.

But it had to be on her terms.

Then he could finally claim her forever.

He dropped his hand from the door.

And made his way back to his lonely bed.

Chapter Twelve

Caterina lay in her bed and stared up at the ceiling.

Midnight.

She couldn't stop thinking about him. Since their kiss in the cellar, she'd realized Rip Savage was the type of man she'd been looking for her whole life. When she opened herself up in Italy and discovered his betrayal, it had been easy to hide behind newly built walls. Falling in love was scary as hell, and her past had not been a success story.

But now that she was back at Winsor, she knew things had changed. By being forced to start over, they'd strengthened the foundation of their relationship. Every day, he proved his true feelings for her. She woke up every morning excited to see him. She loved talking with him, working with him, and most of all, she saw clearly the man her father had taken in like family.

He'd been right. Rip was a man who had the potential to love passionately and had transformed the winery by pouring in his very heart and soul. It was more than a business to him—it was his livelihood. His creative vision.

His home.

Cat sat up in bed. For the past few nights, she'd allowed herself the space and time to come to terms with the overwhelming truth.

She loved Rip Savage and wanted to marry him.

It was time to finally show him.

She got up from bed, shivering as her bare feet hit the cold floor, and walked over to the adjoining door. Her hand settled on the knob and her heart pounded madly in her chest. Would it be locked? Would he be asleep? Would she have the courage to give him everything she'd been holding back?

Cat dragged in a deep breath and turned the knob.

The door swung open.

"I've been waiting for you."

The gravelly, seductive voice drifted in the air, making her freeze. Her gaze searched the darkness, finally settling on the shadowy figure sitting on the edge of the bed. The hum of sexual energy crackled in the silence. Anticipation flowed through her veins. She moved closer. "I needed to be sure."

He straightened to his full height. His sweat pants hung low on his hips. His chest and feet were bare. Coal-black hair curled around his ears and brushed his neck, the thick strands tousled as if he'd been trying to sleep. The scent of musk and man drifted to her nostrils. His gaze seethed with emotion as he slowly closed the distance between them, stopping right in front of her. "And now? Are you sure?"

Her breath shuddered from her lips. She lifted her hands and placed them on his shoulders. "Yes."

His mouth descended. His lips brushed hers with the lightest of strokes, his tongue gliding along the edges of her mouth in a teasing caress. She rose on tiptoes to get closer, to get more, but he resisted, nibbling on her bottom lip as his tongue slid between her lips for just a taste, then drew back.

"I need the words," he commanded, his hands pulling through her hair, rubbing the strands between his fingers. "I need you to be mine, because without you, this winery means nothing to me anymore. I want you. Want you in my bed, in my life. Want you for my wife. Want you forever. Do you understand?"

Her skin burned. She shook with pure need, her eyes stinging with emotion, and clasped her hands behind his head, arching up. "I want you, too," she breathed out against his damp lips. "I want you to be mine. I want to run the winery with you, and be your lover, and your friend. I want you to be my husband, for us to be a family. Do you understand, Rip Savage? Right now, it's about you and me—nothing else."

His mouth took hers, his tongue plunging deep, claiming her with possessive strokes as he drank, the raw hunger beckoning to her like a primitive mating call. The rough scratch of his stubble rubbed against her cheeks, and she thrust all ten fingers into his midnight hair, holding him with her own demand as she met and matched every stroke of his tongue with her own.

He dragged his mouth from hers and stared into her eyes with a stirring tenderness. Then he bent over and swept her into his arms, carrying her to the bed and laying her on the quilt. Never taking his gaze from her face, he stripped off his sweats and joined her. With quick movements, he pulled the black slip down over her shoulders, releasing her naked breasts, dragging the silky material over her belly, her hips, her legs, then tossing it to the floor. He lay against her, hard muscles pressed against her soft curves. One thigh tangled with hers, holding her open for his touch.

Then he proceeded to fulfill the glittering promise in his eyes as he used his mouth and hands and tongue to push her to the limit of ecstasy. Her breasts were treated to the loving touch of his fingers as he tugged at her nipples and soothed with his tongue. He stroked the flesh of her stomach, her thighs, explored the dip of her belly button and the sensitive crease where hip met thigh.

She was just as greedy to touch him. She tested his hard muscles with her nails, tangling her fingers in the thicket of hair that covered olive-toned skin. She traced the lean strength of his thighs, moving inward, cupping and squeezing his pulsing shaft with loving strokes that made him suck in his breath and jerk his hips. With a growl, he shifted lower, pushing open her thighs, and then she felt his warm breath on her sensitive core. Every muscle tightened with anticipation, her breath coming in ragged gasps, and then his tongue licked her slow and sweet, and she arched into the pillow, begging for more.

He gave it to her. He rubbed her clit with a feather light touch as his tongue explored, pushing her closer to the edge. Curling two fingers, he thrust into her over and over, until he found the spot that made everything inside clench and shiver. His tongue licked her clit and he hit the magic spot and then she was coming hard, his name falling from her lips.

Kissing her gently through the aftershocks, he fit himself with a condom. Then rose up above her and interlaced his fingers with hers. Her dazed gaze met his and his lips tugged in a sensual smile that promised her everything.

"Again."

He surged inside her with one strong, perfect thrust. She gasped at the stretching, tight sensation, her body quivering and clenching down. His fingers squeezing hers, his gaze pinned on her face, he took her on a wild ride where her body met and matched each thrust he demanded. The tension escalated slowly as Rip contrasted long deep strokes with slow, teasing motions, until she was mad for him. The pace increased to a demanding, frantic tempo until she hurled over the edge, screaming from the shattering release. He called out her name as he shuddered and came, his body jerking, hands still holding hers.

They drifted down together in a pile of tangled limbs and sweat-dampened skin.

A long while later, he whispered the words in her ear.

"I love you, Caterina Victoria Winsor."

She smiled in the darkness and stroked his cheek. "And I love you, Ripley Savage."

She closed her eyes with a contented sigh and slept.

Chapter Thirteen

One week later, her father's voice echoed up the stairs. "Delivery for you, sweetheart."

She made her way down, smiling back at him as he placed the vase down on the table. Two dozen red roses gleamed in the sunlight, the ruby soft petals opened in full bloom. She lowered her nose to the bouquet and drew in a deep breath. The sweet scent reminded her of everything she'd once longed for and finally had.

"Going to read the card?" he asked teasingly.

She plucked the small cream envelope from the holder, already knowing what it said.

Presto.

Yes, she thought to herself. *Soon*.

"Are you ready?"

She nodded at her father and followed him outside. The walk down the path was symbolic of the home she'd left and returned to, leading her to the future. The sun shone bright and hot in a cloudless blue sky. The vines and red barns shimmered in the distance against the backdrop of the mountains. A hawk lazily circled above, dipping gracefully, then rising back in flight. Her high heeled Louboutins tapped over the pavement until she reached the high archway and paused in the doorway.

Her gaze lifted and met his. Time slowed. Stopped. Then pushed forward as it always did, bringing her closer. The music rose in the air but every step toward him was at her own pace and her own choice.

Her father kissed her cheek and stepped away. She tilted her chin up and stared at the man she loved. A beautiful smile curved his lips and gleamed in his eyes. She repeated the words with everything she was. He repeated them back with the ring of truth and reverence in his voice.

And then he kissed her like it was the first time, and to Caterina, it was.

The first kiss for the beginning of their lives together as man and wife.

They danced and ate and spoke with guests until the sun hovered in warning. She looked for Rip but he was talking to a large group, so she grabbed a glass of champagne and slipped away.

She walked toward the highest hill which overlooked the winery. Ignoring the pristine white of her dress, she settled on the grass, kicked off her shoes, and watched the glowing orange disk sink slowly over the horizon. The rosy glow of sherbet pinks blended together in a perfect canvas. She sat in silence, soaking in the beauty around her, until she heard him draw near.

She turned to him. He sat beside her on the grass. The elegant cut of his tuxedo emphasized his broad chest and shoulders, moving with each graceful step like a welcoming lover. Jaw cleanly shaven, hair neatly slicked back, he cut an impressive figure. The grin that curved his lips was devastatingly masculine and caused her body to hum. "You look beautiful today."

His gaze traveled over the body-hugging lace of her dress, sweeping over the skin laid bare by the strapless top, the vulnerable nape of her neck exposed by her intricate updo. The naked male satisfaction in her appearance was all too obvious. She smiled back at him with pure joy. "So do you. Tuxedos should be illegal for you to wear. Way too sexy."

"You're my wife."

Her heart softened. "And you're my husband."

The gold band around his finger glinted in the dying sun. He stared out at the valley for a while before he spoke. "When I was young, I never dreamed I could love anyone the way I love you. But more importantly, I never believed someone could love me just as much. Thank you, Caterina. For trusting me with your heart."

Tears stung her eyes. This brooding, strong, defiant man had a heart so big he humbled her. She reached out and took his hand, leaning against his warm strength. "You're my home now, Ripley Savage. And I'll never leave."

They stared out over the valley that belonged to both of them. The vines swayed in the warm breeze and the music drifted in the air, filled with laughter and chatter and celebration.

They sat together, hands entwined, watching the sun set.

Epilogue

One month later

Cat hoisted the box out of the back seat and trudged toward the Salvation Army store. Finally, she'd managed to carve out time and get rid of some old clothes and belongings since her father had moved. The cashier pointed her toward the back for drop-offs, and she chatted with the sweet young girl who helped her remove the items for tagging purposes.

Toward the bottom, her hands closed around the fabric-covered book, and she pulled it out in surprise. Holy crap, she'd forgotten about the love spell. "Do you want me to take that for the book section?" the girl asked.

Cat shook her head. "Actually, I'm going to keep this one, thanks." She slipped it in her purse, finished up, and walked back to the car. Alone, she took out the book again and flipped through the pages. Amused, she remembered how pissed she had been at Earth Mother when Rip had announced they needed to marry. Who would've thought he'd end up being her true soulmate?

The image of her list danced in her mind, and she mentally recited the traits she requested. Huh. Interesting. Rip was everything she'd asked for. How odd.

Even weirder? He'd shown up right after she'd cast the spell. Of course, it had taken her a while to realize he was the one, but was it coincidence he'd appeared in Italy hours after the spell? And what about the strong connection between them? It had been instant attraction, as if it was meant to be. As if Earth Mother had taken care of her but liked to play a few games first.

A chill skated down her spine. She closed the book and tucked it back into her purse. Why did she suddenly feel like she'd dropped into one of her favorite movies, *Practical Magic*? And why did she have this sudden urge to pass it on to the next woman?

Shaking her head at her silliness, she drove to the grocery store to grab a few things, then decided to stop in town and hit the bookstore. Rip had an eclectic taste for books, and she was dying to pick up the new Emma Chase novel. Chase's portrayal of heroes always made her laugh and swoon at the same time, nailing the male perspective with skill.

The bell tinkled merrily as she walked into Bookcrazy and lost herself amidst the shelves of books. The store was well thought out, with interesting nooks and crannies offering readers different experiences. Apple green velvet chairs were comfortably set up, along with a small platform where a poetry night was held and catered to local writers. The delicious scent of paper and vanilla drifted in the air. She grabbed the new Ruth Ware thriller, a political memoir, and Emma Chase's *Getting Schooled*, then headed toward the register.

"Caterina, I haven't seen you in so long! I also hear congratulations are in order—you got married!"

The enthusiastic greeting made her smile as she turned to face the owner, Alexa McKenzie. With her black corkscrew curls and bright blue eyes, she radiated a warmth and energy that made everyone around her happy. Cat hadn't seen her since returning from Italy and missed chatting with her. She reached out and gave the woman a hug. "Yes, the wedding was last month. I'm sorry I haven't come in sooner; things have been crazy."

Alexa rolled her eyes. "Boy, do I understand that. I'm just glad to see you. How's Winsor Winery? And your new hubby—Ripley, right?"

"Yes, everything is wonderful. We're actually hosting weddings now, so let me know if anyone is in need of a new venue."

Alexa squealed with delight. "Why don't you get me some brochures? I can leave them here in the bookshop. I'm so happy for you. You're absolutely glowing."

"Thank you. Sometimes, you have to kiss a lot of frogs to get to Mr. Right." Alexa had known about her humiliation and heartbreak with her ex-fiancé and had encouraged her to take some time away. It was amazing how things could change with time, patience, and the guts to take some chances.

Alexa gave a sigh. "Unless you got the last prince," she said. "I swear, I've tried everything but I can't seem to find any man worth even a second date. I'm losing heart."

Her friend's glum expression reminded her of the frustration of a nice single woman trying to find a worthy man. Almost on cue, her fingers tingled, and she acted on instinct. Cat unzipped her purse and removed the Book of Spells. "Are you up for a more creative way to find Mr. Right?"

Alexa frowned, taking the book. Her fingers drifted over the purple fabric cover. "Cat, what the heck is this? Do not tell me you turned away from Catholicism to the occult?"

She laughed. "No, I found this book when I was in Italy and did the love spell. Crazy, right? Anyway, I know it sounds ridiculous but I met Rip that very night."

Alexa flipped through the pages. "Oh, my God, the fact I'm even considering this shows me I've reached my breaking point."

"Listen, grab a bottle of wine one night and just do it for fun. But when you meet Mr. Right, make sure you get married at Winsor Winery."

Alexa shook her head and laughed. "You have a deal. Here, let me ring you up. And thanks for the book."

"My pleasure." She paused, considering how much to admit. "And, Alexa?"

"Yeah?"

"Don't be surprised if Mr. Right seems to be Mr. Wrong at first. I have a feeling Earth Mother is a complicated entity."

Alexa quirked a brow, obviously confused, but nodded with her usual sunny smile. "Of course."

Caterina bought her books, hugged Alexa goodbye, and headed back to the winery.

Whether it had been the Book of Spells, or her father, or just plain old-fashioned luck and Fate, she was grateful to have met Rip Savage.

She was grateful she'd never given up on love.

The End

* * * *

Also from 1001 Dark Nights and Jennifer Probst, discover Somehow, Some Way and Searching for Mine.

Sign up for the 1001 Dark Nights Newsletter
and be entered to win a Tiffany Key necklace.

There's a contest every month!

Go to www.1001DarkNights.com to subscribe.

As a bonus, all subscribers will receive a free copy of
Discovery Bundle Three
Featuring stories by
Sidney Bristol, Darcy Burke, T. Gephart
Stacey Kennedy, Adriana Locke
JB Salsbury, and Erika Wilde

Discover 1001 Dark Nights Collection Five

Go to www.1001DarkNights.com to subscribe.

BLAZE ERUPTING by Rebecca Zanetti
Scorpius Syndrome/A Brigade Novella

ROUGH RIDE by Kristen Ashley
A Chaos Novella

HAWKYN by Larissa Ione
A Demonica Underworld Novella

RIDE DIRTY by Laura Kaye
A Raven Riders Novella

ROME'S CHANCE by Joanna Wylde
A Reapers MC Novella

THE MARRIAGE ARRANGEMENT by Jennifer Probst
A Marriage to a Billionaire Novella

SURRENDER by Elisabeth Naughton
A House of Sin Novella

INKED NIGHT by Carrie Ann Ryan
A Montgomery Ink Novella

ENVY by Rachel Van Dyken
An Eagle Elite Novella

PROTECTED by Lexi Blake
A Masters and Mercenaries Novella

THE PRINCE by Jennifer L. Armentrout
A Wicked Novella

PLEASE ME by J. Kenner
A Stark Ever After Novella

WOUND TIGHT by Lorelei James
A Rough Riders/Blacktop Cowboys Novella®

STRONG by Kylie Scott
A Stage Dive Novella

DRAGON NIGHT by Donna Grant
A Dark Kings Novella

TEMPTING BROOKE by Kristen Proby
A Big Sky Novella

HAUNTED BE THE HOLIDAYS by Heather Graham
A Krewe of Hunters Novella

CONTROL by K. Bromberg
An Everyday Heroes Novella

HUNKY HEARTBREAKER by Kendall Ryan
A Whiskey Kisses Novella

THE DARKEST CAPTIVE by Gena Showalter
A Lords of the Underworld Novella

Discover 1001 Dark Nights Collection One

Go to www.1001DarkNights.com to subscribe.

FOREVER WICKED by Shayla Black
CRIMSON TWILIGHT by Heather Graham
CAPTURED IN SURRENDER by Liliana Hart
SILENT BITE: A SCANGUARDS WEDDING by Tina Folsom
DUNGEON GAMES by Lexi Blake
AZAGOTH by Larissa Ione
NEED YOU NOW by Lisa Renee Jones
SHOW ME, BABY by Cherise Sinclair
ROPED IN by Lorelei James
TEMPTED BY MIDNIGHT by Lara Adrian
THE FLAME by Christopher Rice
CARESS OF DARKNESS by Julie Kenner

Also from 1001 Dark Nights

TAME ME by J. Kenner

Discover 1001 Dark Nights Collection Two

Go to www.1001DarkNights.com to subscribe.

WICKED WOLF by Carrie Ann Ryan
WHEN IRISH EYES ARE HAUNTING by Heather Graham
EASY WITH YOU by Kristen Proby
MASTER OF FREEDOM by Cherise Sinclair
CARESS OF PLEASURE by Julie Kenner
ADORED by Lexi Blake
HADES by Larissa Ione
RAVAGED by Elisabeth Naughton
DREAM OF YOU by Jennifer L. Armentrout
STRIPPED DOWN by Lorelei James
RAGE/KILLIAN by Alexandra Ivy/Laura Wright
DRAGON KING by Donna Grant
PURE WICKED by Shayla Black
HARD AS STEEL by Laura Kaye
STROKE OF MIDNIGHT by Lara Adrian
ALL HALLOWS EVE by Heather Graham
KISS THE FLAME by Christopher Rice
DARING HER LOVE by Melissa Foster
TEASED by Rebecca Zanetti
THE PROMISE OF SURRENDER by Liliana Hart

Also from 1001 Dark Nights

THE SURRENDER GATE By Christopher Rice
SERVICING THE TARGET By Cherise Sinclair

Discover 1001 Dark Nights Collection Three

Go to www.1001DarkNights.com to subscribe.

Discover 1001 Dark Nights Collection Four

Go to www.1001DarkNights.com to subscribe.

ROCK CHICK REAWAKENING by Kristen Ashley
ADORING INK by Carrie Ann Ryan
SWEET RIVALRY by K. Bromberg
SHADE'S LADY by Joanna Wylde
RAZR by Larissa Ione
ARRANGED by Lexi Blake
TANGLED by Rebecca Zanetti
HOLD ME by J. Kenner
SOMEHOW, SOME WAY by Jennifer Probst
TOO CLOSE TO CALL by Tessa Bailey
HUNTED by Elisabeth Naughton
EYES ON YOU by Laura Kaye
BLADE by Alexandra Ivy/Laura Wright
DRAGON BURN by Donna Grant
TRIPPED OUT by Lorelei James
STUD FINDER by Lauren Blakely
MIDNIGHT UNLEASHED by Lara Adrian
HALLOW BE THE HAUNT by Heather Graham
DIRTY FILTHY FIX by Laurelin Paige
THE BED MATE by Kendall Ryan
PRINCE ROMAN by CD Reiss
NO RESERVATIONS by Kristen Proby
DAWN OF SURRENDER by Liliana Hart

Also from 1001 Dark Nights

Tempt Me by J. Kenner

About Jennifer Probst

Jennifer Probst is the *New York Times*, *USA Today*, and *Wall Street Journal* bestselling author of both sexy and erotic contemporary romance. She was thrilled her novel, *The Marriage Bargain*, was the #6 Bestselling Book on Amazon for 2012, and spent 26 weeks on the *New York Times*. Her work has been translated in over a dozen countries, sold over a million copies, and was dubbed a "romance phenom" by Kirkus Reviews. She makes her home in New York with her sons, husband, two rescue dogs, and a house that never seems to be clean. She loves hearing from all readers! Stop by her website at http://www.jenniferprobst.com for all her upcoming releases, news and street team information. Sign up for her newsletter at www.jenniferprobst.com/newsletter for a chance to win a gift card each month and receive exclusive material and giveaways.

Discover More Jennifer Probst

Somehow, Some Way: A Billionaire Builders Novella
By Jennifer Probst

Bolivar Randy Heart (aka Brady) knows exactly what he wants next in life: the perfect wife. Raised in a strict traditional family household, he seeks a woman who is sweet, conservative, and eager to settle down. With his well-known protective and dominant streak, he needs a woman to offer him balance in a world where he relishes control.

Too bad the newly hired, gorgeous, rehab addict is blasting through all his preconceptions and wrecking his ideals…one nail at a time…

Charlotte Grayson knows who she is and refuses to apologize. Growing up poor made her appreciate the simple things in life, and her new job at Pierce Brothers Construction is perfect to help her carve out a career in renovating houses. When an opportunity to transform a dilapidated house in a dangerous neighborhood pops up, she goes in full throttle. Unfortunately, she's forced to work with the firm's sexy architect who's driving her crazy with his archaic views on women.

Too bad he's beginning to tempt her to take a chance on more than just work…one stroke at a time…

Somehow, some way, they need to work together to renovate a house without killing each other…or surrendering to the white-hot chemistry knocking at the front door.

* * * *

Searching for Mine: A Searching For Novella
By Jennifer Probst

The Ultimate Anti-Hero Meets His Match…

Connor Dunkle knows what he wants in a woman, and it's the three B's. Beauty. Body. Boobs. Other women need not apply. With his good looks and easygoing charm, he's used to getting what he wants—

and who. Until he comes face to face with the one woman who's slowly making his life hell...and enjoying every moment...

Ella Blake is a single mom and a professor at the local Verily College who's climbed up the ranks the hard way. Her ten-year-old son is a constant challenge, and her students are driving her crazy—namely Connor Dunkle, who's failing her class and trying to charm his way into a better grade. Fuming at his chauvinistic tendencies, Ella teaches him the ultimate lesson by giving him a *special* project to help his grade. When sparks fly, neither of them are ready to face their true feelings, but will love teach them the ultimate lesson of all?

The Marriage Bargain

Marriage to a Billionaire
By Jennifer Probst
Now Available

Want to find out where the Book of Spells winds up next? Read *The Marriage Bargain*!

The sizzling first book in the *New York Times* and *USA TODAY* bestselling Marriage to a Billionaire trilogy by "one of the most exciting breakout novelists" (*USA TODAY*) Jennifer Probst.

A marriage in name only...

To save her family home, impulsive bookstore owner, Alexa Maria McKenzie, casts a love spell. But she never planned on conjuring up her best friend's older brother—the powerful man who once shattered her heart. Billionaire Nicholas Ryan doesn't believe in marriage, but in order to inherit his uncle's corporation, he needs a wife and needs one fast. When he discovers his sister's childhood friend is in dire financial straits, he's offers Alexa a bold proposition.

A marriage in name only with certain rules: Avoid entanglement. Keep things all business. Do not fall in love. The arrangement is only for a year so the rules shouldn't be that hard to follow, right? Except fate has a way of upsetting the best-laid plans....

* * * *

CHAPTER 1

She needed a man.

Preferably one with $150,000 to spare.

Alexandria Maria McKenzie stared into the small homemade campfire in the middle of her living room floor and wondered if she had officially lost her mind. She glanced down at the piece of paper in her hand which held all of the qualities she dreamed her soul mate would possess. Loyalty. Intelligence. Humor. A strong sense of family and a love for animals. And a healthy amount of income.

Okay, she had most of her ingredients already cooking. One hair from a male family member. Her brother was still pissed she plucked the strand directly from his head. A mix of scented herbs, probably to soften his male testosterone and give him a tender side. And the small stick for ... well, she hoped that didn't mean what she feared. Let each item simmer in the fire and blend.

With a deep breath, she threw the list into the silver bucket and watched it burn. She felt like an idiot for creating a love spell, but she had no options left and little to lose. As the owner of an eclectic bookstore in a trendy college town, she figured she was allowed some quirks. Like sending up a prayer to Earth Mother to bring the perfect man.

Alexandria rose from her cross legged position and hobbled to the kitchen for a fire extinguisher. The smoke rose and reminded her of the burnt pizza crust on the bottom of her toaster oven. She crinkled her nose, shot the spray in the middle of her carpet, and went to hunt up a glass of red wine to celebrate Saturday night.

They would have to sell Tara.

Her family home.

Alex grabbed a bottle of Cabernet Savignon and thought about her dilemma. Her bookstore was mortgaged to the hilt. Her goal to expand the store into a café would take careful planning and there wasn't a dime to spare. Her gaze swept over the Victorian loft and easily calculated there was nothing to sell. Not even on Ebay.

She was twenty seven and probably should live in a cool condo, with designer clothes and a date every weekend. Instead, she took in homeless dogs from the local shelter and bought a lot of trendy scarves to update her outfits. Alex sighed. She believed in living in the sunlight, being open to every possibility, and following her heart. Unfortunately, none of those traits were currently saleable to save her mother's house.

Alex took a sip of the ruby red liquid and acknowledged there was nothing left to do. No one had the money, and this time when the tax collector came, there wouldn't be a happy ending. She was no Scarlett O'Hara. And Alex didn't think her last ditch attempt to make a love spell to lure the perfect man to her door was going to help.

The doorbell rang.

Her mouth fell open. My God, was it him? Alex looked down at her grungy sweat pants and cropped shirt and wondered if she had time to change. She got up to rummage through the closet, but the knocking sounded impatient, so she walked over, took a deep breath, and reached for the knob.

"About time you answered the door."

Her hopes plummeted. Alex stared at her best friend, Maggie Ryan, and gave a scowl. "You were supposed to be a man."

Maggie snorted and walked in. She waved a hand in the air, flashing perfectly manicured cherry red nails, and flopped down on the sofa. "Yeah, keep dreaming. You scared your last date half to death. I won't be setting you up again. What happened here?"

"I can't tell you. What do you mean I scared him to death? I thought he was going to attack me."

Maggie raised one arched brow. "He leaned in to give you a good-night kiss. You stumbled back and fell on your ass, making him feel like an idiot. People kiss after a date, Al. It's a ritual thing."

Alex tossed the remaining trash into a bag and scooped up the bucket. "He had tons of garlic at dinner and I didn't want him near me," she said.

Maggie grabbed the wine glass and swigged a healthy swallow. She stretched out long legs clad in black leather, and hooked her high heeled boots over the edge of the battered table. "Remind me again why you haven't had sex in the last decade?"

"Witch."

"Celibate."

Alex gave up and laughed. "Okay, you win. Why are you gracing me with your presence on a Saturday night? You look good."

"Thanks. I'm meeting someone for drinks at eleven. Wanna come?"

"On your date?"

Megan made a face and drained the rest of the glass. "You'll be better company. He's a bore."

"Why are you going out with him?"

"He looks good."

Alex dropped next to her on the couch and sighed. "I wish I could be like you, Maggie. Why do I have so many hang-ups?"

"Why don't I have any? So, what's the deal with the fire?"

Alex sighed and confessed. "I was creating a love spell. To get a man."

Her friend threw back her head and laughed. "Okay. Give me the whole story. What were you doing with the bucket?"

"I made a fire to honor the Earth mother."

"Oh, my God."

"Shut up and hear me out. I'm desperate. I still haven't met Mr. Right and another small problem came up I need to solve, so I combined both my needs into one list."

"What kind of list?"

"One of my customers told me she bought this book on love spells, and when she made a list of all the qualities she looked for in a man, he showed up."

Now, Maggie looked interested. "A man appeared in her life with all the things she wanted?"

"Yep. The list has to be specific. It can't be too general, or supposedly the universe gets confused with your desires and sends nothing. She said if you follow the spell, the right man will appear."

Maggie's cat green eyes gleamed. "Let me see the book."

Alex tossed her the little fabric covered book. Suddenly, she felt less like an idiot. Nothing like another single female to make you feel better about the quest for a man, she thought to herself. She waited for Maggie's opinion.

"Pretty cool. Show me your list."

Alex waved off her request. "I burned it."

"I know you have another copy under your bed. Forget it, I'll get the thing myself." Her friend stalked off toward the canary yellow futon and stuck her hand under the cushions. Within seconds, her list was held triumphantly between bright red fingernails, and Maggie licked her lips as if she was about to dive into a lusty romance novel. Alex collapsed on the carpet. The humiliation was about to begin.

"Number one," her friend recited. "A Mets fan."

Alex stared at the table. She braced herself for the explosion about to come.

"Baseball!" Maggie shrieked. She waved the paper back and forth in the air for dramatic effect. "Damnit, how can you make your number one priority baseball? They haven't made it to the World Series in years! It's a fact in New York there are more Yankees fans than Mets, and that wipes out half the male population."

Alexandria glared. "The Mets have heart and character, and I need a man who can root for the underdog. I refuse to sleep with a Yankee fan."

"You're hopeless. I give up." Maggie continued. "Number two, loves books, art and poetry." She paused to think about it, then shrugged. "You own a bookstore and you write poetry. I accept. Three, believes in monogamy. Very important to the list. Number four, wants children."Maggie looked up. "How many?"

Alex smiled at the thought. "I'd like three. And if I can't have children, I want to adopt. Should I have specified adoption in the list?"

"No, Earth Mother will get it."

Maggie continued. "Number five, knows how to communicate with a woman. Good one. I'm sick of reading books about Venus and Mars. I've gone through the whole series and I still don't have clue. Number six, loves animals." Maggie groaned. "That's as bad as the Mets!"

Alex scooted around on the carpet to face her. "Is not! If he hates dogs, how can I continue my volunteer program at the shelter? And what if he's a hunter? God, what a nightmare! I'd wake up in the middle of the night and find a dead deer staring at me from over the mantelpiece."

"You're so dramatic."

"The shelters are overcrowded and they try not to destroy. If volunteers take the extras for a few nights, more dogs are saved. They need as much help as possible."

"I've heard the speech before, and no, I'm not volunteering. Dogs cramp my style."

"But--"

"Number seven. Has a moral code of ethics and believes in honesty. Should've been number one on the list, but what the hell, I'm not a Mets fan. Number eight, a good lover." She waggled her eyebrow with interest. "That would be number two on my list. But I'm proud the item even shows up. Maybe you're not as hopeless as I thought."

"Keep going."

"Number nine, has a strong sense of family. Makes sense - you guys remind me of the frikkin Waltons. Okay number ten..." she trailed off. Alex swallowed hard and waited. The clock ticked. She knew her friend read the item again to confirm the validity of the request. "Alex, I think I'm reading number ten wrong."

Alex sighed. "Probably not."

Maggie recited the last request. "Needs $150,000 available cash." She looked up. "I need more details."

Alex met her friend's gaze dead on. "I need a man I can love, with an extra $150,000 thrown in. And I need him fast."

Maggie shook her head like she surfaced from underwater. "For what?"

"To save Tara."

Maggie blinked. "Tara?"

"Yeah, my mother's home. You know, like in the movie, *Gone with the Wind*? Remember how my mom used to joke about needing more cotton to pay the bills? I haven't told you how bad it's gotten, Mags. Mom wants to sell and I can't let her. My whole family lives there, and they'll have nowhere to go. I'll do anything to help, even marry. Just like Scarlett."

Maggie moaned and grabbed her purse. She ripped out her phone and punched in some numbers.

"What are you doing?" Alex asked.

"Canceling my date. Somehow, I think this new item needs to be discussed. Then I'm calling my therapist. She's very good, discreet, and she takes midnight appointments."

Alex laughed. "You're such a good friend, Maggie."

"Yeah, tell me about it."

The Start of Something Good
Stay, Book 1
By Jennifer Probst
Coming June 5, 2018

Discover the brand new STAY series!

War changed him. Betrayal wounded her. But everyone's heart deserves a second chance.

When Ethan Bishop returns to the Hudson Valley, his body and spirit are a little worse for wear. As a former Special Forces paratrooper, he saw his fair share of conflict, and he came home with wounds, inside and out. At his sisters' B & B and farm, he can keep all his pain at a safe distance. But quiet time isn't easy when a fiery woman explodes into his life…

It's business—not pleasure—that brings Manhattan PR agent Mia Thrush reluctantly to the farm. Tightly wound and quick tempered, Mia clashes immediately with the brooding Ethan. Everything about him is irritating—from his lean muscles and piercing blue eyes to his scent of sweat and musk.

But as the summer unfolds and temperatures rise, Ethan and Mia discover how much they have in common: their guarded histories, an uncontrollable desire, and a passion for the future that could heal two broken hearts. But will their pasts threaten their fragile chance at a brand-new future?

On behalf of 1001 Dark Nights,
Liz Berry and M.J. Rose would like to thank ~

Steve Berry
Doug Scofield
Kim Guidroz
Jillian Stein
InkSlinger PR
Dan Slater
Asha Hossain
Chris Graham
Fedora Chen
Kasi Alexander
Jessica Johns
Dylan Stockton
Richard Blake
and Simon Lipskar

Made in the USA
Middletown, DE
01 May 2018